SCATTERED CINDERS

ANGELA CORBETT

Midnight
Sands
Publishing

SCATTERED CINDERS

ANGELA CORBETT

PROLOGUE

My bare feet hit the cold tile floor as I ran down the hall, my toes curling for grip. Star, my little grey kitten with a soft white ring of fur around her neck, was running after a toy ball and we were racing to see who would get to it first. She glanced at me and I returned her determined gaze...right before she abruptly skidded into a stack of pillows. I stopped running and fell into the pillows after her, giggling as I searched for her through the fabric. After a few seconds she emerged from her plush cave, toy in her mouth. She shot me a gloating look before she started to take off back down the hall again, pawing at her ball as she went. I followed her, starting the chase again.

I was cut off by a blur running out in front of me. It was about the size of a ten-year-old boy. I frowned. My cousins, Mark and Kory, were visiting and I'd never gotten along with them. They were two spoiled boys and they both had mean streaks. Mark had run into the hall from where he'd been hiding in one of the bedrooms. A cruel look covered his face as he tackled my sweet Star, grabbing her by the neck. Star started crying in protest. Anger bubbled within me. "Put her down!" I yelled.

Mark's face twisted into a sneer. "No," he said, and pinched Star tighter. Star yelped again and tried to squirm away.

"You're hurting her!"

An awful smile spread on his lips. "I know."

My simmering anger turned to a boil. I loved animals, and Mark was harming mine. That made him my enemy. I loved my kitten more than anything and knew it was my job to protect her. I gave a comforting glance at Star before I turned my eyes on Mark, concentrating on his face. I repeated the word "drop" over and over in my head. My eyes focused with the precision of a laser as a blue light tinted my vision. Within seconds, smoke started percolating around Mark. A glowing blue flame circled his legs and started to flicker. Mark looked down, screamed, and dropped Star. The kitten ran over to me, her little eyes still wide with terror. I scooped her up into my arms, holding her like a baby as Mark started yelling, "You burned me! You *burned* me! I'm telling!"

Mark ran off. I didn't care. Star was safe and that's all that mattered. But I'd only meant to scare him, not burn him. A twinge of regret wound through me and I pushed my brows together at the emotion. Mark had hurt Star, and he would have kept hurting her. He was mean. I'd had to save her. It was my job, and I'd done it. If I'd hurt Mark a little in the process, it was okay because I'd saved Star. I felt better after I'd rationalized it all out in my head.

Mark was a bully and a tattle-tale so I knew I'd have to deal with my parents and uncle soon. That was fine. I hadn't done anything that they could prove. My eye caught a black smudge on the rug. I wrinkled my nose and went to investigate it. A scorch mark. I looked around for something to cover it with and grabbed the curtains in front of the window, adjusting them to hide the mark.

A concert of footsteps sounded down the hardwood hallway and my mom, dad, and uncle Robert came into view, Mark in tow, smiling like the cat who got into the cream.

My dad gave me a reproachful look. "Sweetheart, Mark said you hurt him. Do you want to tell us what happened?"

I steeled myself against my dad's gaze and shot a glare at Mark. "I was playing with Star. Mark jumped out and grabbed her by the neck, and then started being mean to her. She was crying and he was hurting her. So I made him stop."

"You made him stop," my dad said, making it part question, part statement.

I nodded and toed the floor with my bare feet. I didn't like being the center of attention, especially when I was in trouble.

"*How* did you make him stop?" My uncle Robert and Mark's dad asked, his tone a combination of anger and curiosity.

I looked at him and shuddered. Uncle Robert had never been my favorite. He was cold and I hardly ever saw him smile. "I told Mark to drop her."

"And he just dropped her?" Uncle Robert asked, disbelieving.

I lifted my shoulders. "I had to say it a lot."

My uncle hadn't taken his eyes off of me since he started talking. I shifted, uncomfortable with his assessment. "Mark says you burned him."

I had. I wasn't sure how, but ever since I was little, I'd been able to start fires with my mind. I'd never told anyone, but I practiced with my fire when no one could see me. My emotions affected the strength of the flame. Sometimes my emotions got the best of me, and I wasn't as careful. Mark had made me really mad, and he'd been hurting Star so I hadn't been as cautious as usual. My fire was still a secret though—I just had to convince my uncle that I hadn't done anything. I looked up at him with wide eyes. "How would I do that, Uncle? I'm not allowed to play with matches."

My uncle gave me an appraising look, and then his eyes went over my head to my dad's. My dad held his gaze for a moment like my uncle Robert had issued a challenge and my dad was responding with stares instead of words. My dad bent down and took my hand. "I don't know what happened, but it's not okay to hurt someone else. You need to apologize to Mark."

I narrowed my eyes. Mark got hurt because he was hurting my defenseless kitten who hadn't done a thing to him. I was *not* apologizing unless he apologized too. "Mark was hurting Star. Does he have to apologize for that?"

My dad glanced up at my uncle. "Yes, he does."

My eyes went from my dad to my uncle and I watched as my uncle's jaw clenched. "Say you're sorry for hurting the cat, Mark," Uncle Robert said.

Mark scowled and folded his arms across his chest.

"Now," my uncle said in a tone that brokered no argument.

Mark made another face. "Sorry," he said, his voice bordering on mocking.

My dad took my hand, his eyes soft but ringed with authority. "Now it's your turn to apologize, El."

I didn't want to apologize to Mark when I'd done nothing wrong. I'd made him stop hurting my cat. I never would have burned him or hurt him for fun like he'd tried to do with Star. I burned him in kitten-defense, but my explanation wouldn't matter. It took everything in me to say the words, but I knew my parents would insist. "I'm sorry," I said, trying to make it sound like I meant it when I totally didn't.

My dad squeezed my hand.

"I think it's time for us to go. We'll see you soon," my uncle said, putting his hand on Mark's back and guiding him down the hall.

My mom reached down and put her soft hand on my shoulders. "I think you should spend some time in your room thinking about what you did," she said. My dad nodded in agreement and I knew I wouldn't get out of some sort of punishment. My parents both followed my uncle and I went down the hall to my room, leaving the door slightly ajar.

About fifteen minutes later, I heard voices coming from the hall. I snuck to my door and saw my parents standing in the hallway, near where Mark had been tormenting Star. I crept closer so I could hear them, and stood in the shadows, listening to their conversation and watching them.

"There hasn't been a magic user in either of our families for generations," my mom said, worry creasing her forehead. "Why did it have to happen to our little girl?"

My dad bent down, his hands going over the black mark on the carpet that I'd covered with the curtain. He looked up at my mom. "No one can ever know she's a mage, Rose."

My mother sighed, concern lining her forehead. "I know."

My dad reached out his hand and took hers. Her shoulders slumped a bit like his touch had visibly taken away some of her stress. "We'll figure it out."

"How?" My mom asked, her tone sounding defeated. "She's already exhibiting her power. And we have no idea what her power actually is. She starts fires, but is there something more to it?"

My dad stood up and pressed his lips together. "We knew this day might come and we put precautions in place. We won't know the extent of her talents for years. It's something we'll have to figure out with time."

My mom worried her hands together. "We need to teach her to control her magic and keep it a secret."

My dad nodded. "She's smart. We'll explain it and she'll understand."

My mom shook her head as she bit her trembling lip. "If someone knew what she could do—" my mom's voice trailed off and was replaced by a heaving sob.

My dad reached out and pulled her to him, wrapping her in his arms. "They won't find out," he said, his face against her head as he whispered into her ear. "No one will."

I didn't tell my parents my secret—that this wasn't the first time I'd played with my magic fire, practicing it, and trying to get better at controlling it. I knew mages were rare, and those mages who lived in the open often lived in danger. I'd been careful about keeping my powers a secret, but I wasn't certain that I'd always been alone and unseen during my trial sessions. I would have to be more careful in the future; my parents seemed worried.

That night, I climbed into my warm, safe bed in my room, the soft touch of my parents' good night kisses lingering on my cheek. I fell asleep with Star cuddled around my arm, and dreamed of our next adventures.

It was the last time I saw my parents alive.

They were found by our housekeeper on the floor of their bedroom, sprawled out next to each other, my dad's body covering my mom's like he'd tried to shield her. Three streaks of glittering teal that almost looked like claw marks were torn across each of their chests. The same claw marks were also slashed across my bedroom door. Like someone, or something, had tried to get in but for some reason, couldn't.

The police never found my parents' murderers.

But I would.

I'm Cinder, a fire mage, and my flames are fueled by vengeance.

CHAPTER 1

*T*he streets of Everly were quiet as I walked home from my shift at the shelter. I'd been working there for a little over a year. It paid the bills, and kept me safe, which were things I'd learned not to take for granted. I was proud of myself and how far I'd come—on my own, because that's the way it had been ever since I'd run away from my caregiver to save my life.

Memories of what it was like when I was younger and had a home and parents who loved me stabbed at my heart. Now, life was a struggle; I didn't know any other way. I'd struggled at first to find food, then I'd struggled to make money and stay safe. It was in my darkest hour when I finally found my tribe—the people who were like me: magic users in hiding, protecting one another.

The world was full of magic. Some people were open about their abilities. They were the people who came from a long line of magic users and had resources, money, and ways to protect themselves from those who would try to take advantage of their skills. They lived public lives, had huge houses with expensive cars, and were treated like celebrities within the mage community. Others, like me, didn't have any of those advantages and lived in fear of anyone finding out who we actually were, or what we could do. We were constantly looking over our shoulders, hoping someone wouldn't identify us and try to use us. The fear didn't stop me from utilizing my magic for my own purposes and trying to help others, but it made me very careful about who I helped, and who I trusted with my secrets.

Magic is passed down through families at random. No one knows when it will present itself, why, or what the variations of a person's powers might be. One family might produce magic users in every child, another family might skip mages for five generations. And others still, could never have magic at all. Then there were the people who had gone so long between magic users being born in their families that when the power manifested in someone, they didn't realize what it was and often brushed it off as some sort of quirk.

There were several theories about why magic existed, and why some people had it, but others didn't. The idea that made the most sense to me was that for some reason, mages had the ability to tap into a part of the brain that most people couldn't access. Essentially, mages were able to utilize their brain and subconscious in ways that gave them superpowers. Some genetic lines produced offspring more capable of this than others.

In addition to the public world of mages, there was an underground world where magic users were highly sought after, both to hire, and to use. These people wanted to find mages, take them, study them, and harness the magic for their own gain. They would do almost anything to gain access to magic and especially to mages who had a lot of power. When I'd first developed and started playing around with my powers as a child, I hadn't known what my powers were. I'd learned quickly, and also learned that my magic made me prey for some very influential people and I should trust no one.

In the underground, magic users without family and protection were traded and sold like objects. It was horrifying, and something I was constantly aware of, and knew I had to avoid. As soon as I was able, I dedicated my life to finding other magic users who needed protection, and helping them to stay safe. Without the benefit of family, money, and security, we'd had to create our own. My little tribe lived in the tunnels beneath Everly, where the people society didn't want to see, stayed. It was a good place to hide —people like to pretend things that make them uncomfortable don't exist, and burying them in the tunnels is a good way to make that happen. We weren't the only mages hiding there, but mages weren't the most dangerous things lurking in the darkness either. We tried to stick together, and watch out for our own.

"Hi, Kerry," I said, slowing to check on one of my favorite people. He was sitting on a chair outside of his house, watching people come and go.

His eyes lit up when he saw me. "Hadley Scott!" Kerry said. "I haven't seen you for a couple of days."

"I was on a long shift at work."

He nodded and leaned back against his chair, getting comfortable. Kerry was about six feet tall, a burly guy in his fifties with a golden beard, kind eyes, an easy smile, and the frame of a lumberjack. He lived in an old shipping container at the entrance to the tunnels, and acted like a sentinel for everyone who passed through. He knew more about what happened in the tunnels than almost anyone, and he kept me in the loop. He also made sure the people I cared about stayed safe, and that mattered a great deal to me. I handed him some food. I always tried to bring him something on my walk home from work. "How are things

ANGELA CORBETT

today?" I asked, holding out the sandwich I'd grabbed for him.

"Good, good. Sway's been keeping me entertained."

I raised a brow and wondered what she'd been doing... hopefully not playing with her magic in public. She liked to use it to freak people out. It was going to get her in trouble one of these days. "She is pretty entertaining."

"What's this?" Kerry asked, tilting the wrapped sandwich and trying to peer inside at the contents. "Turkey with cheese?" His voice carried a hopeful note.

I nodded. "Your favorite."

His mouth spread into a wide, grateful smile. "You're too good to me."

I shook my head as I kept walking. "Don't be silly. You deserve all the goodness in the world." I gave a little wave as I continued through the maze of tunnels. The tunnels were originally built as ways for stores to have deliveries made to their basements easily without disrupting the businesses. As time went on, the tunnels that offered basement access to the buildings above also became another access point to the businesses and several stores were robbed. As a result, most of the businesses sealed off their basement tunnel access doors long ago, but the tunnels and their various offshoots remained. Some of them even had doors that still opened into the basements of old, abandoned buildings.

One of those buildings was where my people stayed. The door offered an extra layer of protection, but the magic users who resided there were the best defense against any one intruding. Mages alone could be dangerous depending on their powers, but mages working together were a force. The concentration of my friends all in one spot did carry some risks, however. While it gave us more defenses to have multiple mages with various powers in one area, it would also make us a target if anyone was trying to find us. Luckily, the tunnels were full of all kinds of people, and everyone generally kept to themselves and protected those that they knew could help them. I was one of the people others came to for help.

I continued down the tunnel, watching animals that were hiding in the shadows scurry away at my footsteps. Some of the people lingering there in the dark did the same. The realization that they were all scared because they'd been treated poorly in the past squeezed at my heart. I knew what it was like to be afraid and alone. Even though I knew I couldn't save everyone, it didn't stop me from wanting to take them all under my wing and make sure they had refuge and weren't being hurt anymore.

As I came around the corner, I heard voices. The tones were heavy, and sounded menacing. My heart sped up and I stopped walking. I listened for a few more seconds, and then crept forward slowly. Two figures were locked in a fight, arms swinging and legs kicking as they each tried to gain the upper hand. They were grunting and growling as they grappled, and I couldn't tell which one of them was winning. In the blur of movements, I couldn't identify much about them aside from the fact that one of them had blonde hair and the other's hair was a deep black that reminded me of charcoal.

The guy with dark hair twisted, trying to get in a better position and that's when his face came into focus and I lost all train of thought. He had glittering cobalt eyes that contrasted against his tan skin and night sky hair, full lips, a carved jaw, and cheeks that were currently dimpled with strain from the fight. The blonde guy reached his arm around, shifted, and flipped the dark-haired guy over on the ground, hitting the back of his head on the pavement. I winced and hoped he would be okay.

The guy with blonde hair rose with a sharp smile on his face as he towered over his spent opponent. The toothy smile that looked like a row of small daggers in his mouth instead of teeth is what made me recognize him, and my stomach immediately clenched. Grog. He was well-known in the tunnels—a wraith who needed fresh blood to use his magic. Taking the blood from his victims wasn't pretty, or painless. Everyone knew to stay away from Grog. The dark-haired guy must have wandered into the tunnels by accident—or he was just exceptionally stupid. No one was coming to save him. The tunnels had been forgotten by normal law enforcement long ago; we had to police ourselves.

The guy on the ground made a groaning noise and shifted his head. At least he wasn't unconscious. Grog moved into his strike pose and I was racing forward before I'd even made the conscious decision to do it. And I shouldn't be doing it. Using my magic in public with no disguise went against everything I'd taught myself in order to survive. But I couldn't stand by and do nothing while Grog killed someone defenseless. It wasn't in my nature. The guy with dark hair needed help. I would help him.

"Grog," I yelled, rushing toward him, my chestnut brown hair swishing around my shoulders as I ran. I could feel my golden eyes darkening as my adrenaline and anger increased.

He looked up and narrowed his eyes at me. We'd had run-ins before. The guy on the ground focused on me too, his sapphire eyes bright. I willed him to take advantage of the distraction and get up and run. He just laid there, about as helpful as a sack of flour. Maybe he was more hurt than I thought. "Leave him alone," I snarled.

Grog looked from me to the guy on the ground. I could practically see his thoughts moving, and knew just as certainly when he'd made his decision. "No," Grog said. "He's mine."

Grog leaned down, talons that looked like needles stretching from the tips of his fingers. I had mere seconds before he'd push those talons into the man. I stopped about ten feet from Grog, planted my feet, put my hands up in front of me with my palms out facing him, and concentrated all of my attention on the wraith. My vision sharpened and took on a blue hue as flames rose in my irises. I watched as the smoke started to twirl around him.

Grog halted his attack on the man and started yelling at me to stop instead. I just needed him to back off and then I'd let him go before the smoke turned into flames. "Are you done, Grog?"

"No!" he roared, and turned back to the guy on the ground.

I increased the pressure of my magic and in seconds, the smoke that had been circling around him flared to life, flames rising from the ground. Grog screamed and took off down the alley.

I dropped the flames and released a breath I hadn't known I was holding, and then turned my attention to the guy on the ground. He was looking at me. I'm not sure what I'd been expecting as a reaction...relief maybe, perhaps a thank you for not being turned into Grog's dinner. I got neither. The guy's eyes flashed and fury drenched his features. His wrath was totally focused on me. "Why did you do that?" he growled as he pushed himself up off the pavement, his body rising like a finely tuned machine.

I stared at him, stunned. After several seconds, I finally found words, "Are you kidding me? Do you know where you are? Or did you wander into the tunnels by accident?" I pointed toward the alley where Grog had retreated. "That wasn't some random person who lives down here for fun. It was a wraith who needs blood to fuel his magic. He was about to kill you! I saved your life!"

They guy reached down, brushing dirt off of his jeans and black shirt. "I know exactly who that was. And I had it handled." His skin was pulled tight across his face and his tone was very precise. He seemed livid.

I snorted a laugh. "You were on the ground, frozen and helpless."

A muscle ticked by his eye. "I wasn't helpless."

I raised my brows and crossed my arms over my chest. "A toddler would have had more defensive skills than you did."

His shoulders went rigid and his cobalt eyes flared with intensity. He focused on me as he closed the distance between us. In my haste to help save him from having all his blood leeched away, I hadn't totally noticed his aesthetics. He was huge. And I was suddenly very aware of how incredibly attractive this idiot was. His dark hair swept over his forehead in messy chunks. He had a straight nose, full lips, and a jawline that looked like it had been chiseled by a master artist. And all of that sat on top of a body that looked like it was ninety-nine percent muscle and as hard as titanium. I narrowed my eyes. Why did all the hot guys have to be dumb?

He stopped less than a foot in front of me. I glared at his invasion of my space and held my ground. His lips stretched and suddenly, his powerful arms were locked around me, holding me in place. A spark rushed through me at his touch. I immediately explained it away as anger for the arm prison he'd put me in. I looked down to analyze his hold and how I could escape it and got distracted by his thick arms, corded with ropey muscles. I wrinkled my nose at my reaction. That kind of distraction was not an option because number one, this imbecile was ungrateful at best, and dangerous at worst. He was here. In the tunnels, where he clearly didn't belong. He'd been fighting Grog for some unknown but incredibly stupid reason, because you only fought something like Grog if you had no sense, and I couldn't trust that he wasn't insane. And number two, he'd just watched me use my magic and could now identify me—that was *not* a good thing. I'd spent years cultivating disguises and making sure my powers were used as stealthily as possible. The only people who knew who I was, and what I could do, were the people I trusted implicitly. "Let me go," I hissed, wriggling in his hold.

"Oh no," he said, his arms pulling me tighter to him. "You just screwed up everything, and we need to have a chat."

Fear rushed through me. I had no interest in spending any more time with the hot idiot currently trying to abduct me. Someone being able to identify me and turn me over to the Magic Harnessers for ransom was one of my biggest fears. I was not inclined to spend any more time with this stranger who seemed to be more enemy than friend. "I'm not interested in talking."

"Guess how much I care," he said. He voice was deep and his breath hot on my neck. The sensation shot traitorous electricity through me and made me really mad.

The skin on my face pulled tight with anger. "Probably about as much as I do." I lifted my leg and stomped down on his foot as hard as I could. His grip loosened enough that I was able to move my arm and jam my elbow into his side. I heard him groan, and his grip loosened a little more, enough for me to twist out of his grasp. I turned and started to run. Just as I thought I was getting away, he reached out and grabbed my leg and we both went down on the pavement. Hard.

I caught myself before my face hit the ground, but my hands were already burning from the fall. I reached up, brushing the hair out of my eyes and turned to look back at him. He only had my ankle; I could still get away. I started kicking with every bit of strength I had, using my anger at the whole situation as fuel. He couldn't hold on, but some-how, by some ridiculous twist of fate, he managed to grab my shoe. I scrambled away from him, one foot naked. I stared at him, my eyes wide and a baffled look on my face. That jerk took my shoe! I stalled for half a second, wrapping my head around that information and trying to decide my next move. Demand it back? Fight him for it? No. That would be dumb. I'd just outed myself as a powerful magic user to an unfriendly stranger in the tunnels. I wasn't in the mood to stay and fight this barbarian for my footwear. I gave him a glare as I pushed myself off of the ground, got up, and started to run.

My mood was foul as I looked over my shoulder. He was kneeling on the pavement, his expression one I could only describe as grim curiosity as he watched me flee. My heart was pumping with adrenaline and frustration. I was angry at myself for letting my guard down and being identified. And I was furious with the jerk who had done the identifying and, to add insult to injury, took my freaking shoe!

I ran for several blocks, taking paths I normally wouldn't just in case he was following me. When I was certain of my safety, I went home. I came to the curved arch alcove that led to Haven, the building my people stayed in. Ancient red brick crumbled around the foundation. It was hundreds of years old and I was surprised it had held up this well with no real maintenance. The tunnels protected the basements of the buildings from weather though, so that helped. I came to the large metal door, pulled out my keys, and unlocked five different locks. Some might call the security paranoid; I called it thorough. Anyone who thought the locks were overkill hadn't spent much time in the tunnels. I slipped inside, shut the door behind me, and relocked all of the locks. Then I leaned against the back of the door, breathing a sigh of relief.

I thought about the man. Dark hair falling over his face, all hard lines that projected testosterone, full lips that should be illegal on a man, and piercing blue eyes. My mind wandered to his big arms and large hands...hands that had been wrapped around me trying to submit me, and the same hands that had stolen my shoe right off of my foot. I narrowed my eyes at the negative turn of my thoughts, and then welcomed them because it broke the spell I'd been putting myself under about the attractive and dangerous thief.

I furrowed my brow and grumbled under my breath. Now I'd have to find another pair of shoes and I really liked those! Breaking shoes in is hard, especially when you run as much as I do.

CHAPTER 2

*S*way was watching the news and I stood in the doorway, watching behind her. Another terrorist attack, fires destroying hundreds of thousands of acres of land, earthquakes crumbling cities and killing people. She flipped off the news as I sighed and leaned against the exposed brick wall that matched the red brick on the outside of our home. She heard me and turned her head around. "Things keep getting worse," I said, motioning to the TV. I was concerned about the rise of violence I'd seen recently. It felt like we were on the verge of something—something terrible and terrifying. I just didn't know what it was. Part of me wondered if mages might be helping to cause the problems—or fight them. Mages were incredibly powerful and unless they had protection from their families or other magic groups, people kept their powers a secret.

Sway leaned forward and grabbed her drink off the table. She loved soda, and loved it even more when it was flavored with extra sugar. "You worry too much, Hadley," she said, sipping her sugar water as she twisted on the couch so she could see me better.

"Someone has to," I answered, plopping down next to her. "Where is everyone?"

She waved her hand toward the doors. "Out. Perry had a party to go to. Lauren and Lexi had a swim meet, Jeb is working, and Monty had a date."

My eyebrows went up. "Monty had a date?"

"I know," she said, her eyebrows creeping up. "We were all stunned."

"I didn't know he was interested in dating. Who is she? Does she have magic?" I frowned as various scenarios flooded my brain. "Do I need to be worried?"

Sway gave a hefty sigh. "He's fine. He met her at school."

That didn't make me feel much better, but at least I had a way to track her down if he went missing. Abductions were a cruel reality of our world. Unless you had someone protecting you, you had to constantly be on the lookout for people who wanted to use you. Magic Harnessers—people who tried to steal magic and use it for their own purposes— were real, and they were petrifying.

Sway looked at me from the side. "You put everyone else's needs in front of your own. You need to start taking care of yourself first."

I shook my head, snorting a laugh as I realized how much I'd fooled her. Did I like helping other people? Sure. Everyone does. Did I want to make sure people I cared about were safe? Of course I did. But she was making me seem far more altruistic than I was. My main motivation, and the reason for almost every decision I made, was to find the people who had murdered my parents, and kill them. It had become a personal mission that had turned into an obsession the longer it went on without resolution. Someone had taken my family from me, along with my only hope for a normal life, and stolen it. I was on a personal vendetta, and I would get retribution. "I'm not as self-sacrificing as you make it seem."

She shifted and moved to the floor in front of the couch, stretching a leg out. She'd been practicing yoga and karate for years and I seriously envied her flexibility. She bent at the waist and grabbed her foot with her hand and then her face contorted into a weird expression as she inclined her head to look at me. "Why are you only wearing one shoe?" she asked, her tone full of confusion.

I screwed up my face. I was still so shocked by what had happened that I'd forgotten I only had one piece of footwear. The thief's infuriatingly handsome face flashed in my thoughts and I scowled. "It wasn't my choice."

"Whose choice was it?"

I had a slew of colorful names for him, but tried not to swear around my friends who were younger and impressionable. "A jerk's. I met him on the way home in the tunnels on Vine Street. I thought he needed help. Turns out, he didn't. And then the dummy attacked me for trying to save his butt."

She looked as offended by the whole thing as I had been. "That's not very nice. Did you ask him why?"

I pressed my lips into a line. I'd been trying to escape the chat he wanted to have, not prolong it. "He was aggressively persistent about not letting me leave. I decided not to stay and have a discussion."

One of Sway's eyebrows went up and she looked at me like she was seeing something other than what I was trying to project. "Was he hot?"

His dark hair, deep blue eyes, and wide shoulders flashed into my mind. So. Hot. And I wasn't going to admit that to a single soul, ever. I had a hard time even admitting it to myself. "I'm not going to answer that."

Her lips spread into a grin. "So he was *way* hot!" she paused, her head tilting and eyes going up to the ceiling like she was weighing her options. "I think I would have stayed to see where things went."

I waved a hand in front of me like I was giving her permission. "Feel free to try it if you're ever being accosted by a dimwit the size of a gorilla."

She gestured toward my foot. "So why are you walking around half barefoot?"

I narrowed my eyes as the scene replayed in my head. "Because the jerk stole my freaking shoe."

Sway gave me a look. "He *stole* it?"

I nodded.

"Like, off of your foot?" she asked, a wrinkle forming between her brows. "You let him get that close?"

I glared. It wasn't that hard to imagine. Hand-to-hand combat wasn't easy. You used the weapons you had available. "I was trying to get away from him and he grabbed my leg. We both fell. I kicked at him, but he was able to hold onto my foot and pull my shoe off."

She frowned. "Why didn't you take it back?"

"Because he'd seen me use my powers and could identify me. I thought I should get away as soon as possible."

"Why didn't you just start him on fire?"

I'd asked myself that same question. Thanks to my stupid heroics, the stranger knew I had elemental fire magic and he could easily give someone my physical description. I should have neutralized the threat. But I hated hurting people. It wasn't in my nature unless the person had done something to deserve it. I still didn't know what the shoe thief's motives were. "It's a shoe. It wasn't worth the energy."

She rolled her eyes. "You could have just singed him a bit."

I shook my head. "He'd already seen some of my powers. I wasn't going to show him anything else, or give him any additional information."

She made a hmmph noise. "Fair enough. Hopefully you'll never see him again."

I nodded in agreement. "Fingers crossed." A heavy weight seemed to settle on my chest as I said it, and I had a feeling that wouldn't be the case.

It had been three days since the incident with Grog and the shoe thief. Despite feeling like I constantly had to look over my shoulder, which wasn't an unusual feeling for a rogue mage anyway, things had been normal. I'd been busy at the shelter on a forty-eight hour shift. The long shifts always wiped me out and I was happy when I got to go home where I could relax. It was getting colder outside at night so the shelter was overwhelmed with people looking for a hot meal and a warm bed. I hadn't run into Grog since I'd set him on fire, and neither had Sway, Perry, Lauren, Lexi, Jeb, or Monty...that I knew of. I hadn't been home to talk to them, but none of them had texted me about it.

At the entrance to the tunnels, I said hello to Kerry and made my way down the wide pathway. I glanced in the direction of Grog's makeshift house, various metal pieces in different states of decay patched together to make a living space. I didn't see him there, but I still watched my back as I continued to Haven.

I opened all five locks on the front door and breathed in the scent of sugar as I pushed into the house. Someone had been baking something. I shut the door behind me, locking us all in, and walked across the painted concrete floor into the kitchen. I grabbed a chocolate chip cookie off of the counter and broke it apart. The inside was still gooey and the chocolate melty—my favorite. I was about to take a bite when I heard a commotion from somewhere down the hall and I was accosted by Sway, Perry, and Lexi, who came from the other room at a run, and barely stopped before plowing me over.

"Whoa," I said, jumping back and then trying to regain my balance. "What's going on?"

"We met the jerk," Sway said breathlessly, a coy smile playing at her lips.

An uneasy feeling immediately rose in my chest as I asked, "What jerk?"

"The jerk who took your shoe," Lexi answered, wiggling her eyebrows.

"You weren't kidding about him being hot!" Sway reached out like she was touching something invisible and then quickly pulled her hand back like she'd been burned.

I put a piece of cookie in my mouth and it tasted like heaven. "I didn't say he was hot," I mumbled between bites.

Sway rolled her eyes. "You didn't say he wasn't, either."

Lexi started bouncing from foot to foot. "He's been in the tunnels asking about you!"

My eyes widened and the cookie suddenly felt like lead in my stomach. "What do you mean?"

"He brought your shoe," Perry said.

I blinked. "He what?"

"He thought a girl running around with only one shoe might be something people noticed—"

"I *totally* noticed," Sway interjected.

"—and he wanted to find you. We nicknamed him OWWLS," Perry said.

"OWWLS?" I asked.

"For the Old Woman Who Lived in a Shoe," Perry said.

I laughed out loud. "Good grief, I love you guys. I hope you told him that name. And I hope you didn't tell him anything else."

They all looked at me like I was an idiot. "Of course we didn't tell him anything about you," Perry said.

"That would be *so* wrong," Lexi said. Her tone sounded like she'd just eaten something disgusting.

I leaned a hip against the counter. "Did he seriously go through the entire tunnel system asking everyone if they knew a girl missing a shoe?"

Lexi nodded. "I wanted to text you but Sway said not to bother you at work."

Anticipation zinged through me and I immediately quelled the traitor emotion. I had no business being excited about the dangerous idiot who was using my shoe as an identification device. I frowned. Now I'd probably have to change my appearance or something stupid like that. I'd done something similar once before, and didn't look forward to doing it again. I liked my dark brown hair and bright blue eyes. "Well if someone is ever looking for me in the future, feel free to text—even if I'm at work."

Sway eyed me closely and bit the corner of her lip. "Do you know who he is?"

"The shoe thief?" I asked, pushing my brows together. I walked past the three of them to get some milk out of the fridge. "Yeah, he's some guy with an ego and a fondness for feet."

Sway pressed her lips together and shook her head slowly. "He's a lot more than that. Do you have your phone?"

I nodded.

"Do a search for the Oklahoma City tornados two years ago," she said.

I did. She took the phone from me, scrolled through the videos and then clicked one. As the video pulled up, I saw a man standing on the screen and immediately recognized the dark hair and wide shoulders. He was alone in the middle of a city, the sky a strange greenish grey color. A tornado was whirling in front of him; it couldn't have been more than a few blocks away. The entire area looked like it had been deserted as people tried to escape the path of the storm. The shoe thief was in the middle of the road, in the direct path of the tornado. The lines of his face were hard with determination as he raised his arms above him—the same way he'd done the night I'd tried to save him—and faced the storm down. Hair on the back of my neck prickled and I wanted to yell at him to run away. The tornado moved closer and closer and then it abruptly stopped in front of him, like it was a dog obediently listening to commands. Over the course of a few minutes, I watched as the storm started to collapse in on itself, getting smaller and smaller until it had completely dissipated. I stared, dumbfounded. He had stopped a tornado —rain, sleet, and wind—and controlled the weather with nothing more than his magic. And not only had he stopped it, but he'd made it submit to his will. Which meant he was an incredibly powerful mage. I'd never seen anything like it.

"Why wasn't this all over the news?" I asked.

"People thought it was digitally altered," Sway said. "The only people who really believe he did that are those of us who know magic exists—and those who want to use it."

Like the Magic Harnessers. They'd love to get their hands on someone with his power. Imagine what people could do if they could control the weather. It could be used to make tsunamis, hurricanes, tornados, and take out entire cities and states in a covert way because it would seem natural. It could also be used as a profitable venture for everyone from farmers to ski resort owners. And since you can't mess with the weather in one area without it affecting other places as well, it could seriously screw over entire countries and economies. His power was impressive, and he was even more dangerous than I'd originally assumed.

"He's powerful. If he's being this brazen with his magic,

I'm surprised he hasn't been taken by Magic Harnessers. Who is he?" I asked.

"His name is Storm," Sway answered.

Storm. Because he could control the weather. I rolled my eyes. "That's adorable. Did he pick that name himself?" It sounded like something someone with a lot of muscle but not much intellect would do.

"I think it's his given name, but most people don't call him Storm," Sway said. She paused, seeming to choose her words carefully. "His last name is Hurston."

I froze with my glass of milk halfway to my lips, my mouth gaping. "As in *the* Hurstons?"

Sway nodded slowly. "The same. Everyone calls him Charming."

Of course they did. And I'd heard of Charming Hurston and his antics. He was well-known for being an egotistical, self-centered player. I wrinkled my nose, annoyed that I'd tried to help him when he certainly didn't need it, and even more so now that I knew who he really was—a pretty boy with an attitude. "Well, I can attest to the fact that he's anything *but* charming."

"He looks pretty charming," Lexi offered, resting her chin on my shoulder as she looked at my phone and the video paused on his sculpted face. "He's like a real-life prince in the magic world."

She was right about that; the Hurston family was legendary. I bit the corner of my lip and shook my head slightly. Good grief. Of course I'd had to save the notorious Storm Hurston—a man with a super stupid name who could have easily saved himself. Why couldn't I save a normal dude? The Hurstons were one of the most powerful magic families and their lineage went back for centuries—an anomaly since no one really knew how magic was passed genetically and some families skipped having magic users for decades. Shoe-stealing Charming didn't have to worry about being targeted, abducted, or having his magic stolen. He had protections with his family—a lot of them—and people to cater to his every whim. He was basically magic royalty. Which begged the question: what was he doing in the tunnels, fighting a wraith? And why was he looking for me now?

"What did he say when he told you he was looking for me?"

The three of them glanced back and forth at each other like they were trying to decide how to answer.

"Just tell me," I said. "There's no need to sugarcoat it."

"He said it was very important that he find you," Lexi answered carefully.

"Okay, that's not so bad."

"I told him there was a good chance he wouldn't get what he wanted," Perry said.

Nothing wrong with that either. It was true.

Perry gave me an uncertain look. "He said he always gets what he wants. And he wants you."

So that was bad.

Perry kept going, "He said he'd clear the tunnels with a windstorm to get you out if he had to."

And now he was threatening my home, and innocent people, including my friends—the people I viewed as family. Anger punched my chest. So the very *un*-charming Charming was hot, dumb, and had an ego the size of the Arctic. We both had element-based magic. I wondered who would win if we squared off. "I told you he's a massive jerk," I said, tipping my glass toward them.

"But still *super* hot," Sway said dreamily.

A knock sounded on the front door and Perry jumped up. "I'll get it."

"You said he's been looking for me for a couple of days?" I asked Lexi and Sway.

Lexi nodded. "We've all seen him wandering around, holding your shoe like a little lost puppy."

"It wasn't lost," I said, my tone infused with anger, "it was stolen."

"It was stolen after you tried to kick me with it. Repeatedly," a deep, slightly familiar, and irritatingly attractive voice said from behind me. My whole body came to attention and I was intensely annoyed at the betrayal.

I turned and saw him standing in the middle of our kitchen. All muscle, irises I could drown in, and some serious boundary issues. I narrowed my eyes, pushed my shoulders back, and folded my arms across my chest. "I kicked you because you were attacking me and trying to drag me off to whatever cave you crawled out of. I wasn't going with you, shoe or no shoe. What the hell are you doing here?" I asked, then turned to glare at Perry. "Why did you let him in?"

Perry put his hands up in defense. "He said he saw you walk in here and if I didn't let him talk to you, he was going to conjure up some wind and rip our house apart. I decided not to risk it."

If I could have shot daggers at the shoe thief with my eyes, I would have. "I didn't want to talk to you during our last meeting and I told you so. In response, you threatened my friends and our home. Twice. Do you really think that makes me want to talk to you now?"

He gave me a blank look. "I don't care whether you want to talk or not, that's exactly what's going to happen."

Grrrr. He was pompous and entitled, two of the things I hated most. "No." I pointed toward the door. "Get out."

He ignored my command like I hadn't even spoken and it aggravated me even more than I was already aggravated. I hadn't thought that possible.

"I've been looking for you." The frustration was evident in his tone.

Yes. How dare I not come immediately when he'd started wandering around with my shoe in tow. He probably wasn't used to not getting exactly what he wanted, whenever he wanted it. "I've heard."

"And you didn't respond." His voice was tight.

I crossed my arms over my chest. "I know. While my curiosity can get me in trouble sometimes, when I heard some weirdo was wandering around aimlessly, trying to identify me via shoe, I decided that was a path I really didn't need to explore. You could be a serial killer obsessed with feet for all I know."

Dialing up the notorious Charming wasn't a good idea for someone like me. Hearing that he was looking for me hadn't been an invitation, it had been a warning to run. One that I hadn't considered heeding because I'd been running my whole life and I was sick of it. And aside from that, I knew Charming's kind—privileged and arrogant humans who thought the world bowed to them. I wanted nothing to do with him. "I know you're probably not used to this, but not everyone falls all over themselves when you walk into a room."

He cocked a brow and looked thoroughly amused. I wanted to punch him. "Do you know who I am?"

Do I know who he is? Like everyone should fall down at his feet and worship him. I rolled my eyes. "Yeah. You're the ungrateful princess who instead of saying, "Thanks for not letting Grog suck my life away," got pissed, attacked me, and took my property."

"Princess?" he said the word slowly, enunciating each syllable like no one had ever insulted him before. I found that extremely hard to believe.

I nodded. "If the shoe fits. Did it?" I asked, raising a brow.

"Have you been wandering around in my shoe and composing odes to my shoelaces?"

His tongue went over the inside of his cheek as he studied me. "Do you have some sort of deep devotion to your footwear?"

"As a matter of fact, I do. It takes a long time to wear shoes in and those were some of my favorites. Now I only have one of them and blisters from the other shoes I've been wearing since you stole mine. You can give my missing property back any time."

He watched me, assessing for several seconds. "You kicked me with it. I feel like that makes it mine."

"If I'd known you had a foot fixation, I would have kicked you with something bigger."

His eyes flashed with mirth. "And if I'd known you were going to run, I would have captured you faster."

He had no idea what I could do. Someone like him would be so full of themselves that if I unleashed all of my magic, they'd be sick for days—provided they didn't flat out suffer a psychic break. "Try it," I said through my teeth. "I dare you."

His eyes darkened this time. "Next time I capture you, it will be because you want me to."

I managed to look indignant, though his proximity to me and the lines of his shoulders were making that outrage hard to muster. "You're confident."

"Yes. I'm excellent at what I do."

"Ego?"

"No. Magic."

Perry, who was older than Sway and Lexi, coughed. I'd forgotten they were even there. I turned to see the three of them, watching with rapt fascination, like they were seeing a soap opera play out in real time. That was all I needed. Witnesses to this fight. They'd already been here too long. "I need to deal with *un*-Charming. Will you three give us some privacy, please?"

Sway's face fell and Lexi looked like someone had just stolen her puppy. I sent my eyes to the ceiling and shooed them off, hoping they'd respect my wishes and not just eavesdrop down the hall. They sulked out of the room. I had no idea why Charming had been looking for me, but I didn't want my friends to be concerned with it. If it was something they needed to know, I'd tell them.

I turned my attention back to our visitor. His lips slid into an amused expression.

"Why are you looking at me like that?" I asked, warily.

"Because you called me Charming. So you *do* know who I am."

Of all the conceited... "First, I called you *un-Charming*. Second, don't flatter yourself. I had no clue who you were until my friends told me you'd been here threatening them while I was at work during the past couple of days and they recognized you. Until thirty minutes ago, the only thing I knew about you was that you were the most aggravating and bristly human being I'd ever met. My initial assessment of you was spot-on. Why are you here, and what do you want?"

He leaned against the kitchen countertop and studied me for several seconds. "We have a mutual enemy, Hadley."

Great. So someone had told him my name—or the name I used at least. I'd taken on a new identity after I'd run away and no one knew my real name.

I raised my brows. A mutual enemy was news to me. "You don't even know me. How do you know who my enemies are, or that we share one?"

He licked his lips and my eyes couldn't help but follow the movement. They lingered there a little too long before snapping back up to meet his gaze. He grinned, totally aware

31

of the affect he was having on me. "Your reputation precedes you," he said.

I thinned my eyes. That sounded ominous. "What reputation is that?"

He studied me, his eyes full of interest—for what, I wasn't sure. "I know about the fire on Clayborne Avenue, and the inferno on Green Street. There were others too, but those are off the top of my head. It took me a few hours to put things together, but I did. You're Cinder, the arsonist, and you're practically a legend."

I pursed my lips and my heart sped up. I'd been careful to keep my identity a secret my whole life, and then I threw it all away by fighting Grog in front of Charming. I hadn't taken my usual precautions and now I was paying for it. Anger at my own stupidity coursed through me. The fires on Clayborne and Green had both happened when I was younger and still trying to learn to control my magic. I'd had years of practice and now when I burned something down, I was more underhanded about it—and made sure I wasn't ever caught. Cinder was a name the press had given me, but no one had ever identified me in person. I was careful to take out any video feeds, and to keep myself covered with a hooded cape so I couldn't be easily recognized. I wasn't about to tell him any of that though. I simply stayed silent, not wanting to give anything away.

"On Clayborne, you destroyed a sweatshop. On Green Street, you stopped a human trafficking ring."

I'd been given a gift and had decided long ago to use it for good, as well as for my own purposes. No one was injured in the fires on Clayborne and Green, or in any of my other incidents, but I wouldn't have felt too bad if the people exploiting others *had* been hurt. They were bad people doing bad things and I was happy to have the chance to stop them. But again, not information I needed to share with Charming so I kept my features neutral and said nothing.

He leaned against the counter, the seams of his shirt straining around his biceps. "It was noble," he said, admiration in his voice. "I was impressed."

I rolled my eyes. "I imagine someone like you is always impressed with destruction."

"No," he said, watching me closely. "Power. Few people in the world use it for good. You appear to be one of them. And I'd like you to help me take down someone completely vile."

I arched one of my eyebrows. "Who would that be?"

His eyes narrowed and he stared at the wall, his mind going to a totally different place than the photo of the beach he seemed to be focused on. "I don't know. That's why I need you."

He didn't know? What the... "You don't know? It sounds like you need a private investigator."

The crease between his eyes deepened. "We already have those. They're not helping."

"Okay. Then why me?"

He looked directly into my eyes and the sincerity there was unmistakable. "Because you're exceptionally powerful, and I need the help of another strong elemental mage. Your magic would work well with mine in a fight."

Technically, rain could put out my fire, but his wind could also fuel it. He was right though; I was powerful—more powerful than he knew, that was certain. But the Hurstons had all the money and connections in the world. I couldn't understand how one more mage like me, a rogue mage at that, could be of any help. Surely they had strong fire mage friends. "What do you need my help with?"

He sat on one of the chairs in front of the countertop and looked down for a minute before answering. When he did, his voice was soft, "My sister, Sarah, was abducted last week.

My family is doing everything in their power to get her back, but we're not getting far, and we have very few clues. She was out with two friends. Her friends are now dead. Their bodies were recovered in the same place where her phone last logged her location. Her body wasn't left with the others, so we believe she's still alive. The only clue we have about the person who took her is that there were three streaks of glittering teal that almost looked like claw marks across both of her friends' chests." I managed to hold back my gasp, but it was several seconds before I remembered to breathe again. He'd just described the same marks as the ones that had been found in my house and on my parents the night they were murdered. I'd been looking for someone with information about what had happened to them for years. Now Charming was looking for the same person who had killed my family and he was asking for my help to find them. This was the closest I'd ever been to being able to reveal who, or what, had taken my parents from me.

"So you were in the tunnels trying to get information when I saw you the other night?"

"Yes."

"From Grog?" I asked, a note of doubt in my tone.

"Grog is known for having information if you pay the right price."

That was true, but the price usually came in a very unpleasant and deadly form. "He would have drained you dry before he ever gave you the information you wanted."

"I was willing to take that risk to get my sister home safe."

It was a stupid idea. His parents would have ended up with two dead kids that way. "That was risky, and wouldn't have played out well for you."

He met my eyes, cold and hard. "I had it under control, and I would have stopped him before anything serious happened to me."

"You would have *tried*," I said, my tone implying that he would have been very unsuccessful in the attempt.

"He'd already told me some information before you arrived."

That piqued my interest. "Like what?"

Charming shifted and grabbed a cookie off the counter. "That the person I'm looking for will be at the Mystic Ball this weekend. I need to find them. And I need a date who can help me do that." He looked up at me, his eyes darkening, "Preferably one who burns hot."

I raised my brows at that, certain he was referencing my magic, not the fact that he thought I was attractive. I didn't keep up with magic circle gossip, but from the little I had heard, Charming was a known player who dated incredibly beautiful women. He wasn't interested in me for anything other than help finding his sister. And I was considering using him for help finding the person who killed my parents. I needed to keep reminding myself of that.

The Mystic Ball was an expensive and ornate party held by magic's most elite every year. Charming would have never missed it because the Hurston family was one of the most highly respected magic families in the world. I'd heard about the ball, but I'd definitely never been invited. I didn't even know where it was held. Now Charming was asking me to go with him? I really hoped I wouldn't have to dance. "What makes you believe Grog's information?"

He took another bite of cookie. "Because Grog traffics in information. Plus, I paid him well for it and threatened him if he gave me incorrect intel." Of course he did. Because threats were second nature to someone with the power, money, and magic lineage Charming had. "My family is employing an investigation team, and I'm helping to facilitate their queries by getting as much additional information as possible. The information we have so far points to the fact that this involves someone, or maybe several people, in the magic community. We can't go to any of our family friends and mages we know for help. We can't trust them."

I almost snorted a laugh. "But you think you can trust me? You don't even know me."

He looked at me, pulling his bottom lip back with his teeth. I reminded myself not to stare. "Yes. I think I can. You haven't been part of the mage culture. You've grown your magic outside of it, not getting influenced by the politics. I don't know your story, but I imagine there's a reason for why you are where you are, and why you feel the need to help others, whether it be taking out a sweatshop, helping a stranger who seems like they're about to be killed by Grog, or simply finding other magic users in need of a home and shelter. You use your magic for good, and there's no one better than my sister. She needs help and I can't go to anyone else. Will you help me?" Charming asked. His eyes were soft and his voice sincere. It would be easy to fall for someone like that. Luckily, he wasn't always this endearing.

I furrowed my brow and looked at him closely, trying to ascertain the best course of action. Partnering with him would mean putting myself out there and risking my own life. More people would find out about my magic, and I didn't have the protections Charming did. I'd spent my whole life trying to stop that from happening, and keep people from finding out about my powers. And it wasn't just me I had to think about. I had no way to keep all of my friends safe from the Magic Harnessers. I didn't want them to become targets as well. But Charming had every resource on the planet available to him. There was a chance he could keep us all safe.

Previously, I had wondered who would win if we squared off. Now I wondered what would happen if we used our magic to work together. Could we really do it without killing each other? I wasn't sure. But this was also a huge opportunity for me. It was the closest I'd ever been to finding out who had murdered my parents. Charming had information and could get me into places I couldn't get to alone.

"My home, and my friends and I would all need protection from the Magic Harnessers."

"Done," he said immediately. "I can take care of that."

"What about after this is all over? How can I guarantee we'll have the security we need going forward once people know about my magic?"

"I'll have a security team put on you just like my family has. You won't have to worry."

"Indefinitely?"

He nodded.

Being rich and powerful sure made things easier. I wondered what that life would be like.

"What about the security team that was assigned to your sister?"

"She wasn't considered high risk and only had one guard. We've changed protocol now. Your team will keep you and your friends safe."

So the security obstacle was out of the way; I tried to consider if there were any others. I could only see one; it involved his sparkling blue eyes, alluring smirk, and the thick muscles that encased his frame—and that wasn't a problem I was ever going to tell him about. I'd just have to deal with the attraction on my own. This was my very best chance for being able to find the people who had killed my parents, and I wasn't going to pass it up because I was distracted by the circumference of his arms.

"Give me my shoe back, and we have a deal."

His lips slid into a slow smile. "Done," he said. "I'll send you a dress."

I shook my head. "I can get my own."

"You're sure?"

"I've been dressing myself for twenty-five years, I think I can manage."

He opened his mouth to say something undoubtedly snarky, and then closed it. Wise choice.

"Then I'll see you on Saturday." He handed me my shoe.

I took it, and hoped I'd made the right choice. If I hadn't, everyone I loved and everything I'd built could be at risk.

CHAPTER 3

a box addressed to me showed up on the doorstep the next afternoon. I took it inside and opened it. Another silver box with a pretty pale blue bow wrapped around it sat inside. I untied the bow and then gently lifted the top off of the box and gasped. A dazzling new pair of shoes. They were see-through with a three inch heel, pointed toe, and they glittered with blue and silver speckles sprinkled over the entire shoe. They almost looked like glass sparkling in the sunlight. I took them out of the box and slipped them on my feet, trying them out. They felt like I was walking on a cloud and they were a perfect fit. I stood in front of the full length mirror in the hall, putting my foot out and admiring the gorgeous slippers. A smile curved my lips. They had to be from Charming. He was the only one who knew I was going to the ball. At least he'd done something useful with my shoe and figured out my shoe size. I wrinkled my nose at the memory of the shoe theft and considered not taking the gift, but decided it was a peace offering. At least, that's how I was justifying it so I could keep the magnificent heels. Shoes were kind of my weakness. I loved them, and rarely had the money to buy a pretty pair, or the opportunity to wear them. I had one now.

"Holy crap!" Sway said, as she walked into the room with Lauren and Lexi. "Those shoes are amazing! Where did you get them?"

"I think Charming sent them," I said, turning to examine them from a different angle. I couldn't stop staring at my new glittery gift, and already loved them more than cake—which was *a lot*.

"Why?" Lauren asked, leaning against the wall. She hadn't been at home when Charming had arrived, but everyone in the house had heard about his Haven invasion.

"For the Mystic Ball."

All three sets of their eyes went as wide as saucers. "You're going to the *ball*?" Sway asked.

I nodded, and slipped the shoes off, placing them back in the box gently.

Three identical squeals came out of their mouths! "Oh my gosh! What are you going to wear?" Lauren asked.

"It has to be something exquisite!" Lexi said.

"Oh, it will be. Just leave that to me," Sway promised. Sway's magic gave her the incredible ability to weave illusions. They didn't last forever, but she was a master of clothing design, and she could conjure a heart-stoppingly beautiful gown out of thin air.

"You would do that for me?" I asked. I was more than grateful because despite my assurances to Charming, I really didn't have the time or the money to find a gown that would work for such a formal occasion. Charming had offered to send me one, but I hated relying on other people, and who knew what kind of dress he would have procured.

"Don't be silly," Sway said, waving me off like I would be crazy to think she wouldn't do it. "Of course I will. I would love to! You're going to be the most beautiful girl at the ball. You'll stop people in their tracks!"

My stomach clenched at the thought. I'd spent so many years trying not to be noticed that the thought of the magic masses seeing me, and someone possibly recognizing me, gave me serious anxiety. The worry started to spread and I immediately tamped it down with the thought of my parents. This was my opportunity. I might be able to avenge them soon, and if so, then this would all be worth it. And I had Charming's security crew to help keep us safe. Plus, it wasn't like I was helpless—as long as I wasn't up against a mage who could counter my powers.

Sway picked up one of my pretty, sparkling slippers and studied it. "Yes," she said, tilting her head and looking it over, "I can definitely make something that goes beautifully with these. You have to give him credit, he knows how to pick shoes."

I had to agree with her on that. I loved them.

Sway put her fingers to her lips, a small smile playing over them. I'll be back later. I have a dress to design.

I watched her walk away, a slight thrill going through me. I'd never been to a ball. I'd never even really been on a date. My whole life had been a series of firefights, trying to make sure I could survive, and trying to help others survive while I attempted to find the murderer of my parents. Getting dressed up and going out, even if there was an agenda behind it, made me excited and giddy. For the first time in years, I felt like I might be running toward something instead of away from it.

"Stop fiddling with the lace," Sway admonished as she

41

brushed my hand away from the intricate scallops framing my sweetheart neckline.

We were in the car on our way to the address Charming had texted me earlier in the day. He'd sent a fancy SUV with a driver who was part of his security team to pick us up. When my friends in Haven had heard about the plan to help Charming find his sister, and possibly help me find the person who killed my parents, they'd all wanted to come along. I'd managed to keep the guest list to Sway and Perry. Bringing an entire platoon with me would draw unnecessary attention, not to mention that showing up at the Mystic Ball was basically a declaration of your magic power. At eighteen and nineteen respectively, Sway and Perry were the oldest of my friends, and had control over their powers. They were adults, and could make their own choices. I knew they could defend themselves and, to be honest, I felt more confident having them by my side. Sway was wearing an emerald dress that highlighted her curves and brought out her fiery hair. Perry had on a black tuxedo that managed to somehow make him seem less intimidating. He was six-foot-six so that was hard to do. I imagined Sway's magic had helped make that illusion happen.

I looked down at the fabric encasing my figure and still couldn't believe I was wearing it. My dress was incredible! I'd never felt so beautiful, or so self-conscious. It was form-fitting in a way I didn't think dresses could even be. I felt like I'd been sewn into it from my chest to my hips. I was worried that if I bent wrong, I'd break the seams. The gown flared out from my hips into billowy yards of satin and lace. The train trailed behind me like waves on the ocean.

"I've never worn anything like this before," I said, uncomfortably.

"Which is ridiculous because you were *made* for this

dress!" Sway said, rolling her eyes. "You're drop dead gorgeous!"

I wrinkled my nose as I looked down at the pretty, dark blue lace overlaying a shimmering pale blue gown. The sleeves hung off my shoulders and the neckline showed a hint of my chest, emphasizing a brilliant square sapphire dangling from my neck. My earrings matched the necklace, and the colors all combined to bring out the blue of my eyes. My dark hair was curled and swept to the side so it hung over my right shoulder, and my makeup was a masterpiece of grey and pink shades, and incredible contouring. I'd barely recognized myself when I'd turned around and looked in the mirror an hour ago.

"I feel beautiful," I said, and didn't like the taste in my mouth that came with the admission. "It makes me uneasy," I admitted.

Sway gave me a look. "Good! You *should* feel beautiful because you *are*!"

I shook my head. "You're just good at illusion, and you're being nice."

Sway rolled her eyes so hard I thought they might roll out of their sockets, and swung her head to Perry. "Am I just being nice, Perry?"

Perry looked at me appreciatively. "She's definitely not being nice. Charming's going to lose it."

Sway giggled. "He totally is."

This time I rolled me eyes, fidgeting my hands in my lap. "He won't even notice." Did I want him to notice? I kind of did. But what did that mean? Okay, so I was attracted to the guy. I was adult enough to be honest with myself and admit it. He was an attractive guy. And what girl *wouldn't* want to be wanted? I was sure that was all it was. I wanted someone to look at me with desire and it wouldn't matter if it was

43

Charming or some stranger on the dance floor. I felt better after my little internal assessment.

Perry snorted. "Oh, he'll notice. *Everyone* will notice. You'd have to be blind not to."

That reminder made me worried all over again. I knew coming tonight meant that I was putting myself out there and I, and my magic, wouldn't be a secret anymore. The people I'd run away from years ago would be able to find me again. I was older now and more capable, but it still left a knot in my stomach. I had Charming's word that he'd keep me, my friends, and Haven protected. I had no reason not to trust that. But I'd been hiding for so long that it was hard to just flip a switch and be okay with my magic going public.

We pulled up to the hotel the Mystic Ball was being held in. The building was a masterpiece of Victorian architecture. As we walked inside the lobby, a chandelier bigger than my entire bedroom hung from the ceiling. Every piece of furniture was antique, and probably cost a small fortune. The walls were wrapped in flocked wallpaper and the place practically dripped money. I took a deep breath, feeling totally out of my element. I needed to get over that because we had a job to do.

We walked into the hallway leading to the ballroom and were stopped at the door by a woman in a black formal dress. "Name, please?"

"We're guests of Storm Hurston," I answered.

She gave me an appraising look. I must have passed her test because she looked down at her list. "Ah, yes. He's listed with a plus three. Can I have your names for the announcement?"

"Announcement?" I asked, confused.

"Yes, we announce everyone when they walk into the ball."

I froze, unsure about what to say. Sway and Perry both

gave her their names and started through the door before looking back at me. I'd known going into this that people might realize who I was, but I hadn't planned on using my magic, or even my name. The goal was to get in, get the information we needed, and get out. But now it was more than that. If I gave my real name, everyone would know. I'd been in hiding ever since I'd run away to save my life. I wasn't sure if revealing my name was a good idea. My parents were dead, but there were others who still might be looking for me. At some point, the rumors would spread and the news would get back to people that I was still alive. I wasn't ready to let them know my real name, so I used the name I'd taken after I'd gone into hiding. "Hadley Scott." Hadley was my mom's middle name, and Scott was my dad's middle name. I couldn't keep using the name they'd given me, but this made me feel like I still had a piece of them as part of me.

She nodded, wrote down my name, and directed us through the doors. We stood in a line behind a curtain until our names were called. Sway and Perry went first, then the announcer said, "Hadley Scott." I walked into the room and stood at the top of the stairs, my heart racing. I pasted a fake smile on my face as I took in the ornately decorated room. The ceiling was drenched with flowers in various shades of pink. Crystals woven through the blooms glinted off of carefully placed lights. The flowers on the tables mirrored the flowers on the ceiling, only they were in round, slender vases with glass stems so thin I wasn't sure how they were holding the sheer weight of the arrangements. The room smelled like a spring garden, and looked like one too. It was the most spectacular space I'd ever been in, and I couldn't believe I was there—and couldn't imagine how much the décor had cost. It wasn't until I'd stopped staring at the room that I realized how quiet the crowd had become. I looked around and everyone had stopped what they were doing, their eyes focused on me. I couldn't have been more uncomfortable if I'd been standing there naked. My eyes swept the room, a multitude of gowns and tuxedos, faces that seemed familiar and some that didn't, staring back at me, assessing, judging. Magic users were celebrities within the mage world, so it wasn't a surprise that some of them would look familiar, but it was a surprise that any of them would ever be interested in me.

My eyes went over the crowd, searching for a friendly face. That's when I found him. My gaze halted like I'd been going a hundred miles an hour and suddenly hit the brakes. In the middle of the room, with a look of pure longing etched on his face, stood Charming. He was wearing a black tuxedo with a white shirt and cuff links that sparkled like diamonds—and probably were. He started up the stairs to greet me and when he reached the landing I almost gasped. His eyes looked like they were heated from within. "You look stunning," he said, whispering in my ear as he offered me his arm.

"Thank you," I murmured back, still feeling like this was all a dream. I put my hand in the crook of his elbow and let him guide me down the stairs.

Sway and Perry were waiting at the bottom. "You remember my friends," I said to Charming.

He nodded. "Thank you for coming."

"Thanks for inviting us. Just kidding, you didn't," Sway said, a hint of annoyance in her tone. "But thanks for getting us tickets after Hadley asked you to."

His eyes flashed with mirth that didn't seem entirely friendly. "You're welcome."

Sway met his gaze, totally unafraid and unwilling to stand down.

The hush was still lingering over the crowd and people

hadn't stopped staring. Charming's interest in me hadn't helped that. I needed to change the subject before Sway said something she shouldn't and someone overheard. "Your family isn't here tonight?" I asked Charming.

He turned his attention back to me and shook his head. "My parents and our entire security team have been working non-stop trying to find out more information about where my sister might be. But since we can't trust other mages, we haven't gone public with the news of her disappearance. The Hurston family is old in the magic world, and needed representation at the ball, so I was the best choice. Since I had the intel from Grog that this is where I needed to be, we decided to have me cover the ball."

The orchestra at the front of the room started playing a beautiful song. The melody was one I remembered my mom humming during my childhood. It brought back beautiful memories of her sitting by my bed at night, reading me a bedtime stories, and then humming as she lightly brushed my cheek with her soft fingers until I fell asleep. I yearned for those days, and often felt sad when I thought of the things we were both missing out on now. Growing up without a mother's guidance was difficult.

Storm noticed me watching the orchestra, my body swaying slightly to the music as I remembered my past. "Would you like to dance?" he asked.

Surprise washed over my face. I hadn't expected to actually dance. I'd thought we were just here to do a job. "I would love to, but shouldn't we be looking for the person who took your sister?"

He gave me a wink. "We will be."

"By dancing?" I asked.

He nodded, a smile playing at the corners of his lips, and took my hand pulling me onto the dance floor.

Sway and Perry grinned like fools behind me as I looked

back at them over my shoulder. Everyone was watching us—
the notorious Charming and the new girl in blue.

Charming reached around me, his hand like a warm
compress on my back. His eyes were soft and I could easily
get lost in them and be happy—for a while at least. Then
reality would come and I'd remember we were from two
very different worlds and Charming would bring me nothing
but heartbreak.

I looked around the room as we turned, trying to see if
there was anyone I recognized and could name. This was a
gathering of magic's elite; I should know some of them, or at
least know *of* them. Aside from trying to place faces, I was
checking for one person in particular. "Are you looking for
someone?" Charming asked, watching me.

I turned my attention back to him. "Not anyone in particular, exactly."

The fact was that I actually was looking for someone. My
uncle. I hadn't seen him in years, and had no idea if he'd be
here. He didn't have magic—that I knew about, but he was
associated with magic users, and there was a chance he could
show up at the ball. If he did, and if he recognized me,
Charming's security team was going to earn their paychecks.

"Not anyone particular, exactly?" Charming repeated, a
question in his voice.

I lifted a shoulder, trying to make it seem like it wasn't a
big deal but in reality, my heart was hammering a drum beat
against my chest. "My uncle. There's a chance he could be
here."

"And you don't get along with him?"

"No," I said flatly.

Charming's eyebrow went up like he wanted the rest of
the story. I didn't want to go into that much detail.

"We haven't seen each other in years," I said. "Not since I
was a child."

Charming cocked his head to the side and spun me around expertly before pulling me back to him. "Why not?"

"A multitude of reasons." I'd been in the throes of grief, a child desperate to understand what had happened to her parents, and struggling to deal with the realization that I'd never see them again when I'd found out that I would be living with my uncle and his sons, Mark and Kory—the same son who had tortured my little cat, Star. I hadn't stayed there long. The memories tasted bitter as I tried them out on my tongue, and quickly decided not to probe for more.

He nodded and we kept dancing. "I see my family frequently. Family is a big deal for the Hurstons."

I looked at him. "Congratulations." I tried not to let the words bother me. I hadn't had the luxury of a family until I'd created my own through my friends.

"Sometimes it's nice," he said, not picking up on my mood. "Other times it's annoying. But I love them."

Why was he telling me this?

"Do you want a family of your own someday?"

I stared, taken aback. "That's a really random and personal question. We hardly even know each other."

He lifted a shoulder in a half shrug. "Which is why I asked. I'm trying to get to know you." His lips formed a crooked, disarming smile that I didn't trust for a second. "It's just a question."

I considered it. I hadn't ever really thought about having a family of my own. My goal had always been to help people, and get revenge. Dating, relationships, family... those were things I'd never had the time to even contemplate. I didn't believe family meant blood. I'd created my own family, one that I loved very much. "I have my family. Sway, Perry, and all of my friends who live with me at Haven. They're the people who have been there for me most of my life. They'd take a bullet for me, and I'd do the same for them. It's a family I chose, and they make me happy."

He nodded, considering that. "But you could choose your partner as well, and have a family that included everyone."

Yes, I could. And maybe someday I would, but I hadn't really had a chance to think about relationships. I'd been too busy trying to survive my entire life, and keep my friends alive. "I haven't had much time to date, so that's not really on my radar."

"Do you want it to be?" he asked point blank.

I furrowed my brow and thought about it as we moved around the floor. I didn't know what I wanted. The only thing I'd ever been certain of was that I needed to find my parents' killers. "Maybe someday. I'm not sure."

He eyed me. "What's stopping you?"

I lifted a shoulder. "I have too many people I'm responsible for to take the time for me and my wants."

"Ah," he said, his tongue running slowly over his lips. "I can see how that would be difficult. But now you have a dedicated security team to help with some of that responsibility." He spun me again and this time when he pulled me back into him, I could feel every line of his body against my own. My heart sped up and he leaned in to whisper in my ear, "So maybe you need to make some changes."

My heart was thumping in my chest and I felt like I was in some weird twilight zone. The notorious Charming Hurston was interested in *me*? It was too unbelievable to comprehend. And then my bafflement abruptly turned to annoyance. Who did this attractive weather controlling mage think he was? Giving me life and love advice like he had some special insight into the secrets of the universe even though he wasn't much older than I was and he'd never had to struggle a day in his life. Just the other day he'd been stealing my shoe and infuriating me to no end! At what point did our relationship merge into him acting like he wanted to be my friend, and maybe even more than that? I tried to trace it and couldn't figure it out.

The air shifted slightly and Charming and I both looked up, noticing the change, but unable to pinpoint it. "Come on," Charming said, moving his hand from my back and lacing his fingers through mine.

He led me out the door into a beautiful garden area. A maze of flowers and leafy trees stretched before us, dotted by tiny lights that looked like fireflies flitting through the greenery. An asphalt walkway marked a path to navigate the gardens. I breathed in the fresh air. It was so much cooler outside, and I relished the breeze, though I was a little confused about why we weren't inside, trying to find out who took his sister. "Why are we out here?"

"Because I'm counting on the fact that the people we're looking for will follow us."

I stared at him. "Why do you think they'll do that?"

"Because the people who took my sister were interested in her magic. You're stunning, intriguing, and new and shiny. You wouldn't be here without magic and they'll want to know more about who you are, and what you can do."

"So you're using me." It was more of a statement than a question, but I was using him too.

"I think we're using each other." His eyes dropped, snagging on my lips. "They won't be able to resist you. I can't."

My cheeks pinked and I rolled my eyes to try and cover it. "You're being ridiculous."

He held my gaze, his eyes clear and focused. "I'm being honest."

I stared at him, trying to decide if he was really being sincere. I didn't see deception in his expression; instead I was faced with heat, focus, and determination. A flutter started in my stomach and the energy around us seemed to change. He moved closer to me, his hand still entwined with mine. His other hand came up and brushed the side of my cheek. I closed my eyes, reveling in the warmth of his touch and the feel of his body so close to mine. If he tried to kiss me now, I wasn't sure I'd have the self-control to stop him. And I wasn't sure I even wanted to.

"This isn't a good idea," I said, my voice soft.

"Mmm," he answered back, his fingers trailing along my collarbone. "Why is that."

"It would complicate things."

His lips slid into a slow, lazy smile. "I don't mind complicated."

A tingle ran over my lips and I licked them, trying to stop the anticipation. Charming's eyes caught on the movement. "My life is complicated enough."

"It doesn't have to be," he said, his voice gentle. "Let me help with that."

I blinked. The offer stunned me. I'd been on my own, responsible for so many people and taking care of myself for so long that the idea of having someone help me was hard to even wrap my head around.

"I have a lot of responsibilities."

He reached his hand up, a warm weight against the back of my neck and head. He leaned in, his eyes totally focused on mine. His lips were a hairsbreadth away as he whispered, "Let me help you." His mouth closed over mine, electricity flowing between us. His lips were silky soft as they moved with mine in a graceful dance, creating their own kind of magic. It was like the two of us were merging, our energies becoming one. I'd never felt like this before...I'd never wanted anyone. I hadn't allowed myself to want, or need, or think beyond my goals of vengeance. But I wanted this, and wanted him. Badly. And it was terrifying. Whatever this was felt a lot like need. I didn't want to need anyone. I'd built my life on being alone and not having to depend on anyone because last time I'd relied on other people, they'd been taken from me. I couldn't handle that heartbreak again. I pulled away.

"What's wrong," he asked, his hands resting on my waist as his eyes searched mine.

"I can't," I said, stepping back, away from his touch. Severing the connection felt like a knife slicing through me. I looked down and wished my life were different and I didn't have to stop this thing between us before it even really started. "This won't work."

"Why?"

Because it couldn't. Because I'd just had a glimpse into what my life could have been. I *wanted* a partner, and companion, and best friend I could always count on. I wanted this too much and it would break me when Charming inevitably left to go charm someone else and I was on my own again. I'd been broken before. I could get through it. But I wasn't going to put myself in that position willingly. "We're too different."

Emotion feathered across his face. "That's one of the reasons I want this...want you. You're different, and I love that about you. I love your fire, your independence, your fierce soul. I want it all. I want you, Hadley."

He'd just basically said he loved me. No one had ever told me that—not since I was a child. My heart constricted at his words. I wanted that too. Everything he'd said was perfect. But a relationship with Charming couldn't last. It wouldn't, and I knew it. I wouldn't do that to myself.

I shook my head slightly, and his jaw tightened. I could see that he was getting ready to launch into another speech that would try to make me reconsider. He might succeed.

"Hadley—"

I let my eyes fall to the floor and in that moment, the

material of my dress shimmered. The beautiful gown Sway had made for me with her magic started to falter. "Oh no," I gasped.

"What is it?" Charming asked, worry lining his face.

"It's Sway," I said, pointing to the lace that was fading in and out in color from sapphire to white. "Something must have happened to her. She made the dress and her magic is weakening. She's either in distress, or someone is siphoning her power."

CHAPTER 4

J reached down and picked up the gown so I could run, and took off into the ballroom. Charming followed behind me, right on my heels. I needed to figure out where Sway was. People stared as we ran out of the ballroom into the hallway. I'd always had a strange connection to my friends. I could feel them when they were around, I just needed to center myself and concentrate. I stopped in an arched alcove of the giant building and closed my eyes, breathing in and out slowly and rhythmically. After about a minute, I felt pulled down the hall. I followed my instinct and Charming followed me.

We turned down another hallway, then opened a door and went into a corridor. We were getting closer, I could feel it. That's was when I heard an urgent whisper from a room to the side of us. "Hadley!"

I swung my head in the direction of the noise. It was Perry. I ran and hugged him, so grateful he was there, safe, and unharmed. I never wanted to let him go. "What happened?"

He shook his head, his face sheathed with worry. "Sway

was asked to dance by a few different guys. One of them seemed to like her a lot. Some guy named Mark." The hair on the back of my neck stood straight up and I tried not to over-react. There were a lot of Marks in the world. It couldn't be the same Mark I knew—my cousin. "Everyone saw us walk in with you, and then you left with Charming which made people even more curious. Everyone wanted to know who you were, and we were getting a lot of attention." I was angry with myself. I shouldn't have ever left them alone. Charming had thought we'd draw the bad guys out into the garden; instead, they'd zeroed in on our friends.

"Where was our security team?" I asked Perry, and slid my eyes to Charming whose face was also pulled tight with concern.

"All but one of them followed you out into the garden," Perry said.

"They probably thought we were the bigger targets," Charming said, grimacing. "I thought we were too."

So had I.

"The guy who stayed with us was monitoring us, but someone came up and distracted him. I don't think he saw Sway or I leave."

Charming's eyes narrowed and I could tell he was unhappy. "I'm sorry. I promised you safety and my security team screwed up. I will handle this after we find Sway."

I was frustrated, but mistakes happen. It sounded like this abduction was planned. The security guy had been distracted on purpose so that Sway could be taken. "Mistakes happen and I'm sure distracting him was part of the plan." I turned to Perry and asked, "What happened next?"

"Mark offered to take Sway to get a drink. I had a weird feeling about him, so I discreetly followed behind them. As they were walking away, another guy Mark had been hanging out with started following him too. Mark led Sway here, and then they all went into this room." He pointed to the large French doors in front of us. "I've been trying to decide how to attack. I thought about finding you, but I didn't want to risk the chance of them leaving and me not knowing where they'd gone. I'm a good fighter, but I don't know how many people are in there, and you know my magic doesn't work quickly."

Perry's magic was pretty incredible but the side effects hit people later. He was smart to not go in there alone. "You did the right thing," I reassured him.

I turned to Charming. "We know we have at least two people in there with Sway. Maybe more. Are you ready for this?"

Charming gave me an amused look. "I won't have a problem." And with that, he kicked open the door, his magic pushing out and the air spiraling around him like a hurricane he could control with laser precision.

We walked in to see Sway sitting in a chair, being held against her will by two men I hated with my whole soul: my cousins Mark and Kory. They were taller now, and they'd filled out, but their beady eyes and disgusting smirks were exactly the same as I remembered. Sway's face was a study in condensed rage, and I knew she was itching to get up and use some of her karate skills on them both. I would have happily paid to watch that fight, and would have liked participating in it even more.

Mark and Kory each gave me a terrible smile that was so awful I immediately wanted to wash their gazes off. "Long time no see, El."

"Yes," another deep, familiar, and horrifying voice said from the other side of the room. My head swiveled in his direction at the same time my stomach knotted.

I froze, paralyzed at the sight of him. My uncle, Robert Dodd. The man I'd run away from years ago, and hoped I'd never have to see again. My whole body ached with rage and fear as my mind raced. I was going to be sick—but not until I stopped Robert, Mark and Kory.

My uncle gave me an appraising look. "You turned into quite the lovely young lady. I see you changed your hair. It used to be long and blonde, like your mother's." I'd changed my entire appearance when I'd run away because I knew he'd be looking for me. My skin crawled at his visual appraisal and his words. "In fact, I wouldn't have known it was you at all if it wasn't for your name." He shook his head slightly. "You're pretty, but you never were the smartest. Using your mom and dad's names to create your fake name was a poor choice, El.

The more he spoke, the angrier I became. My real name was Ella Hart, and it made me furious that he'd used my nickname. That name was a name my parents had lovingly chosen and used. He wasn't allowed to use it too.

"Do you have any idea how long I searched for you?" he asked. "Years, Ella. Every time news about a fire mage came through the gossip circles, I would increase my efforts with the hope that we could find you, but you covered your tracks well. Until now. Thanks for making it so easy for me. Had I known I just had to take someone you cared about, I would have made more of an effort to keep your parents alive."

Blood drained from my face and I felt like I'd been stabbed. I knew my parents had been murdered by someone heartless, but I hadn't guessed that they'd been murdered by a family member. There couldn't be a worse betrayal. I felt faint and the icy prickles of shock started to set in. At the same time, I felt Charming's hand on my back, steadying me. His touch grounded me with support and I came back to the present. No. This was not happening again. I was not losing another person I loved. I would deal with my uncle and the revelation of who murdered my parents, but not until I saved Sway.

I wanted to kill him, slowly and with a lot of pain. But right now he was deliberately using my emotion to try and distract me. I couldn't let that happen. "Let her go," I growled through my teeth.

His eyes flashed with challenge and his lips lifted in a terrible way. "Come with me, and I will."

"No," Charming said, stepping forward. His voice was solid and brokered no argument.

My uncle laughed like Charming's denial was the funniest thing he'd ever heard. "Do you really think you can stop me from getting what I want, Hurston? Trust me, you can't. And neither can your family's security team and investigators combing everywhere from the tunnels in the city to the forest surrounding Everly looking for your sister."

Charming's eyes hardened with fury and he looked like he wanted to commit murder. "How do you know about my sister, the security team, and the investigation?" he asked, his voice dangerously soft.

My uncle lifted his shoulders. "Your sister has been missing for days. Everyone knows about it."

Charming eyed him. "No, they don't. We've told very few people and only our security team knows about the rescue efforts, or where the searches are taking place."

My uncle's lips spread into a smile that showed his teeth, and they looked ready to bite something in half. "Maybe your team isn't as loyal as you thought. I know a lot of things."

Charming's face morphed into a blank mask. It was the same face I'd seen him make in the tornado video right before he'd forced the twister to crumble into nothing. "Do you know where my sister, Sarah, is?"

My uncle lifted a shoulder in a half shrug. "I might."

Charming's hands clenched into fists and the air around

him started whipping into a frenzy. I stepped back, trying to shield myself from some of the wind. "Tell me," Charming said through his teeth.

My uncle inclined his head in my direction. "Give me your girlfriend, and I will."

Anger flashed across Charming's face. He was absolutely seething. "You're the lowest form of human scum that has ever lived, Dodd. People aren't things. They're not made to be traded or given to anyone."

My uncle gave him a bored look. "Do you want to see your sister again, or not?"

Charming's expression shifted, determination mingling with fury. "If you think you can fight me, you're an idiot."

My uncle's lips curled into a twisted, evil smile. "Let's see how much of an idiot I am."

The air around us started to shimmer and in seconds, there were at least fifty versions of my uncle surrounding us, all smiling the same, evil smile. I couldn't tell the difference between them, and couldn't figure out who was the real one. My uncle didn't have magic of his own, and had always been angry about his lack of power. Since he wasn't born with magic, this meant he'd harnessed his magic from some other mage, in his own personal Jekyll and Hyde lab—something he'd been trying to perfect for years. Either that, or he'd paid the Magic Harnessers a great deal of money to transfer magic to him.

"Who did you steal your magic from, Robert?" I asked, my eyes going around the room and trying to pinpoint who my real uncle was.

All fifty versions of my uncle laughed, creating a vile concert of noise. "A better question would be: who didn't I steal from? I've had goals for a long time. You know that, El. If you hadn't run away, I'd have your magic too."

Memories of my past and that awful lab sprung into my

head and threatened to cripple me. I couldn't let that happen. I dug down into the well of anger that consumed me and pulled from the fury, determined to use my rage for fuel.

The fifty versions of my uncle all spoke at once. "I knew you had magic. So did your parents, but they weren't concerned until the night you tried to start poor Mark on fire after he was just playing with your cat.

"He wasn't playing with her," I snarled. "He was torturing her."

Robert shrugged. "Tomato, tomahto. When Mark came to tell us what you'd done, your parents were worried and discussed sending you to a school for mages so you could learn how to use your powers. That just wouldn't do for my needs. You were clearly a powerful mage to be able to use your magic at such a young age, and with no training. I knew if you were sent away, you'd be protected and I'd never have the chance to take your power from you. So I sent a shifter to abduct you, one known for his fierce protective instincts— because I didn't want you to come to me dead and useless— and one who was also incredibly strong and powerful. My shifter tried to get into your room that night, but couldn't. Someone had put an exceptionally powerful protection spell on your door. When shifters can't complete a task, they get angry. So it went looking for another way to reach its goal. It found your parents and killed them instead. It was an unfortunate turn of events. I would have just as soon preferred to only take you and leave your parents alive, but it all worked out. Once your parents died, I became your legal guardian and got you anyway, like a gift from the universe wrapped up in a pretty little bow. In retrospect, I could have saved myself a lot of time and trouble by just killing them to begin with."

I stared at him, bile rolling in my stomach and wrath rising in my throat. "My parents' lives weren't things you could just discard."

He gave me a condescending look. "But I did."

My blood felt like it was boiling. I'd never been so angry in my life. I wanted to reach over and rip his heart out of his chest. I'd have to settle for burning him to death. If I could kill him twice, I would. We needed to save Sway and Sarah so I could.

He'd chosen the wrong mage to play his illusion game with. He didn't know the extent of my magic, but his trick was about to become useless. Fury surged within me; anger at my uncle for what he'd done, and how he'd ruined my life in multiple ways. Anger that he was trying to hurt Sarah in the same way he'd hurt me, and anger that he was threatening my friends and using them as a bargaining chip.

All of the versions of my uncle lifted their arms, pushing Sway toward my cousins, and the two of them took off, holding Sway's arms and legs so she couldn't wrestle away. Perry tried to catch them and Charming tried to slam the doors shut, but they were both a second too late. I wanted to take off after them and save Sway, but I couldn't. I had to stay and fight my uncle. I was the only one who could.

I focused my anger back on Robert, and all fifty copies of him. Flames danced in my eyes and blue fire burst around each version of him, surging up like a spiral around them. His face was a mask of anger, and as the fire continued, growing hotter, some of the anger was replaced with uncertainty and fear. The various fake Uncle Roberts' started popping out of existence as soon as they got too hot.

Charming held the doors shut with his magic to make sure no one else could get in or out. My uncle wasn't leaving here unless one of us let him.

I heard a creaking noise and looked up. Another chandelier hung above us, just like the massive one in the lobby. And it started to sway. Violently. Charming wasn't paying any attention to it.

"Storm!" I yelled, panic ringing in my voice. I pointed up and watched as the chandelier snapped. It all happened in slow motion.

Without even looking Storm *moved*, pulling me with him as he twisted out of the way of the chandelier, and raising his arms at the same time. A gust of wind came out of nowhere and captured the chandelier, setting it down gently on the floor. If it had crashed, we would have been crushed and the glass would have shattered, slicing us all.

Charming and I looked at each other, relief washing over both of our faces. Perry stood off to the side of us, his eyes wide with shock. I turned back to my uncle Robert, and my breath caught in my throat. One of the doors was wide open and he was gone. "Where is he?" I asked.

Fury radiated from Charming. "I couldn't hold the doors and the chandelier at the same time. He must have realized that and escaped."

My heart sank at Charming's words. I'd brought my friends with me and put them in danger, and now they were in even worse danger and it was my fault. I needed to do something to fix this, but had no idea where to even begin. I didn't know where they'd gone, or what they planned to do with Sway. I'd failed to protect the people I loved the most. How could I right such a massive wrong?

I looked around the room at the shattered glass, torn curtains, and destroyed furniture, and came to terms with reality. My uncle and cousins were gone. And so was my friend. I collapsed on the floor, my head in my hands.

CHAPTER 5

My emotions were all over the place, despair and anger, hopelessness and determination. One minute I wanted to sob into my hands, the next minute I wanted to use them to fight my uncle and cousins until we were all bloody and I'd stopped them from hurting any other person ever again. Sway was my family, and now my uncle had her. He'd taken my family before, and now he was doing it again. I had no idea what he wanted Sway for, other than leverage. He wanted me, undoubtedly for my magic—he'd always wanted it—and hostages were helpful in getting your way. Knowing he had Sway brought back every horrible memory of losing my parents. And now I knew that I'd lost my parents and Sway to the same man—but Sway wasn't dead yet. That was the thought that pulled me from my despair. I would find Sway and I would fight to get her back because there was no way I was letting that malevolent man take any of my family members again.

I got up, steel in my eyes, resolve coursing through me. I wouldn't let them have Sway, or anyone else. "Come on," I said, motioning for Charming and Perry to follow me.

"Where are we going?" Perry asked.

Charming was looking at something on his phone as he ran next to me. "We had a security team outside the hotel. They saw Sway in a car with your uncle and cousins as it sped out of the parking lot. My team has eyes on their vehicle. We're following, and we'll know where they're going."

Charming's security team was handy to have around. I already had a suspicion about where they were headed, however. It was a place that haunted my nightmares. When my uncle found out I had magical powers, he'd been incredibly jealous. He'd always wanted magic, and wanted his sons to have it too. They didn't, but I did. He'd built a makeshift magic siphoning lab in the basement of his vacation home. It was only about an hour from the city, nestled into a quiet piece of land by the beach, and it was rarely used unless he needed it for his own nefarious purposes. He'd tried to take my magic there repeatedly with his own resources. And when it hadn't worked—because of his lack of experience stealing magic and my sheer anger and will, he'd decided to send me to the Magic Harnessers so they could take it for him. Magic siphoning was dangerous, painful, and often killed the mage the magic was being stolen from. I refused to let that happen to me. When I'd found out my uncle's plans to send me to the Magic Harnessers, I'd decided to run away to save my life. I'd never shown my uncle the extent of my magic—but I would tonight.

"I think he's taking her to his magic siphoning lab in the basement of his vacation home. I'm almost certain of it." I said as we got to Charming's car, a black Escalade with chrome trim. It shined like a diamond and practically screamed money.

"He has his own lab?" Charming asked, stunned. He got in the front seat and I jumped in the passenger side. Perry got in the back.

We sped out of the parking lot with Charming following the directions that were being sent to his phone from his team.

I nodded. "He wanted his own magic, and wanted his sons to have it too. None of them did."

"What about your aunt?"

"She didn't have magic either."

"Where is she now?" Charming asked.

"She died when my cousins were young."

"Of what?"

I'd never actually been sure. "They told us it was an accident, but now I wonder if that was really the case. She was a kind woman, but she wouldn't have stood for my uncle's magic obsession. My uncle is a lunatic and I wouldn't put murder past him. I don't remember her well because I was only four when she passed away."

Charming's eyes hardened and his anger seemed to be building even more. "I have no tolerance for people who hurt others."

Neither did I; I'd spent my life fighting against it.

I had a good idea of why my uncle wanted Sway—to use as a bargaining tool to get to me, but I still wasn't sure how Charming's sister fit into this, or what Robert wanted from her. "Why does he want Sarah?"

He pressed his lips together and slid a glance toward me, then to Perry. "If I tell you this, it has to stay between us."

I nodded in agreement and Perry shrugged and nodded as well.

Charming's grip on the wheel tightened, his knuckles going white. "She has a unique magic. Our family has kept it a secret for years, but she used it to help someone a month ago and we weren't able to completely contain the information."

"What is her power?"

He took a deep breath and then answered, "She makes the transfer of magic seamless."

I stared at him. "You mean she can perform a magic transfer on people without any Harnesser intervention?"

He nodded slowly.

"How long does the transfer take?"

"It's immediate."

I gaped at him.

"What's the success rate?"

"One hundred percent."

My mouth fell open even more. The transfer of magic had become a science that had been learned through years of trial and error. A gifted Magic Harnesser could control the amount of magic being taken, and most Magic Harnessers could take magic from mages and transfer it to others, but the process was long—days depending on the amount of power and type of magic being transferred—and painful, and it didn't always take. If his sister's magic had the ability to make the transfer of magic quick, easy, and painless, that could change everything. Everyone would want her...especially people like my uncle.

"That explains why my uncle took her," I said. "He doesn't have magic of his own and he's been trying to get it for years. I wouldn't be surprised if he hired his own Magic Harnesser. Whatever we saw back there in the ballroom with the multiple copies of him was the result of a Magic Harnesser giving him that ability. If he has your sister, his powers could be limitless. He's had her for a week. I'm surprised he hasn't already forced a transfer."

Charming shook his head. "Her power only works if she's willing." His phone rang and he picked it up. "Good. We'll wait for your signal and then follow." He hung up.

Charming pulled to the side of the road a few blocks from my uncle's vacation house and came to a stop behind another black SUV that held some of his security team. It was a road I'd been on many times, and the memories of coming here and enduring the torture my uncle put me through while he tried to take my magic made my stomach clench.

"We're stopping here in case your uncle has his own surveillance. My team is already on the way to check out the perimeter, and we'll follow as soon as we get the call."

I nodded and tried to keep myself from going insane with worry. Less than five minutes later, Charming's phone buzzed and we started toward the house with Charming's security team.

They motioned us to the front door where we crept inside behind several armed guards. I looked around and remembered every part of the house. Not much had changed in the twelve years since I'd been here last. The compartmentalized layout was the same, and so was the décor, a mix of modern and classic. A layer of dust covered the surfaces of the furniture and the air smelled musty and stale. The home wasn't used much. One of the guys pointed to the stairs and we formed a single file line, quietly following them down.

When we got to the bottom, we were in an empty, large room. I pointed down the hall toward the back of the house. There was a door there that opened up into a large lab. In any other house, it would have been four separate bedrooms, but my uncle had made it into one large, horrible room of torture.

We could hear voices coming from inside. There were at least four people in there: my uncle, Mark, Kory, and Sway. I hoped Sarah was in there too.

The lead on the security team motioned for us to move. We did and he took a few steps back to get some velocity behind him, then ran and kicked the door as hard as he could. The door frame splintered and the door swung open as all of Charming's team pushed inside and we followed.

The whole thing took seconds and as we descended on them, my uncle and cousin's faces were priceless, their mouths frozen open in shock.

Sway was tied to a chair, next to another girl who was also tied and hooked up to a multitude of wires. I heard a sound that could only be described as a growl come from Charming as he surveyed the room and his eyes landed on the two girls. The girl next to Sway was surely Sarah.

Charming motioned to his team and they moved forward like they were one person instead of ten, each movement precisely choreographed.

"I don't think so," my uncle said. He raised his arms and a transparent wall seemed to build between him and us. Charming's men ran toward it and were stopped in their tracks. They tried kicking and punching it, but nothing happened. One of them took his gun and shot at a corner, in an area where it wouldn't affect anyone if the shot bounced off the wall. The bullet hit the wall and dropped straight to the ground. My uncle laughed with victory, confidant he'd won this fight.

The anger that had been boiling inside me was back, and getting hotter. I couldn't let this horrible man win. Who knew what damage he'd already done to Sarah. I walked to the edge of the wall, examining it.

"There's nothing you can do, El," my uncle taunted. "The wall can't be penetrated by fire."

I looked at him and smiled slowly, danger glinting in my eyes. Fire wasn't my only trick.

I lifted my arms, palms out and focused every bit of my intention on my uncle and that wall. Flames started in my eyes, white hot, and then they began to build around the wall. I focused on the wall, testing a theory—my uncle's magic wasn't real. It was stolen from other people and even though magic could be transferred, it was never as strong as when the original magic holder used it. My uncle's magic was as fake as he was, and nothing more than an illusion he'd constructed. I specialized in burning up those falsities and I knew that I could do it to him too. The flames burned hotter and my uncle's face grew more and more concerned. The top of the wall started to crumble. I'd stripped him of the illusion and as soon as I did, the wall fell, scattering into hundreds of cinders smoldering on the ground, awaiting my next instructions.

My uncle's mouth fell open and he seemed paralyzed with shock.

"You never did know the extent of my magic, Robert. I never let you see it." Blue fire filtered my vision and his face became a mask of terror and awe. My voice came out as a roar, "I'll let you see it now."

I twisted my wrist, guiding the cinders toward him, circling him, their tiny pieces glowing with anticipation.

"My fire burns away illusions and I can see a person's true nature and reflect it back to them. Their true nature is a culmination of all the things they've done and lied to themselves about…things they've convinced themselves are true. I gather their illusions and the lies they've composed about who they think they are, and pull them away from the person. When that happens, the illusion bursts into flames. The cinders fall, turn to glass, and reflect the person's true selves back at them. They are the things people know deep down, but can't face. It often causes them to have a psychotic break because most people can't handle the truth." I eyed him. "I have a feeling you'll be one of those people, Uncle. Why don't we find out?"

With that, I let the fire rise. It burst up into a column of sapphire flames that consumed him. He screamed, a sharp, piercing noise, not from the pain of the fire, but from the pain of being stripped of the fallacies he'd composed about who he thought he was.

As the fire died down, the ashes fell and the glass reflected his true self back at him. He was an ugly, horrible man with a heart as black as tar. Everyone's mirror was different; some were words, some were images, sometimes it was a combination of both. Words started forming in the glass. Murderer, kidnapper, liar, thief...all things he knew about himself, but refused to own or see the truth in.

My uncle's face crumpled into a defeated mess and he fell to the ground in a ball, sobbing. He was a broken man and I felt no remorse for making him feel that way.

Charming rushed forward to his sister and yanked the wires off her body. Perry ran to Sway and untied the ropes. Sway looked ready to kill someone. "Let me at him," she snarled.

Perry shook his head. "I don't think that's a good idea."

"It's an *excellent* idea," she growled. "Let me go!"

Mark and Kory started to move toward us, anger fanning their faces. Before they could take more than a few steps they both fell to the ground clutching their stomachs, their faces contorting in serious pain.

Perry's eyebrow went up. "Guess my magic kicked in faster than usual."

Perry's magic basically turned him into the karma police. Depending on how a person had lived their life, his magic could be a good thing, or a very bad one. He was able to make someone accountable for their own actions, and make them feel the emotions they'd caused others to feel. Based on how my cousins were writhing on the floor, Mark and Kory had a lot to make up for.

As soon as Sarah was untangled, she jumped up from the chair and grabbed onto Charming as tears leaked from her eyes. He wrapped her in a huge hug, his expression full of love and relief. "I'm so glad we found you," Charming said.

"Me too," Sarah said. "I wanted to kill that jerk."

"I don't think anyone would have minded if you did," one of the security guys said.

He took his mask off and I blinked. "Kerry?" I said, my voice baffled and my expression completely stunned.

His lips spread into a kind smile. "Good thing I gave you those shoes at the ball or I might not have found you."

I stared at him, dumbfounded. "You're the one who gave me the shoes?"

"Course I am. They were spelled so I'd be able to keep track of you. Did you think this knucklehead sent them?" Kerry asked, nodding toward Charming.

I looked between them. "Yeah, I kind of did."

The corner of Kerry's lips went up in a playful smile. "He has no taste. He would have bought you something awful."

"Hey!" Charming said, punching him playfully in the shoulder. "Be nice."

I was so confused. "Do you work for Charming?"

Kerry shook his head. "No, but we know each other. When he was wandering around the tunnels like a lost puppy with your shoe, I pointed him in the right direction."

Charming rolled his eyes. "I wasn't acting like a lost puppy."

Kerry put his thumb and forefinger up about an inch apart from each other. "A little."

I still didn't understand. "So you knew I was going to the ball with him? And you just decided to leave your tunnel post and join his security team for the night?"

Kerry lifted his shoulders. "Well, it's kind of in my job description."

"What's your job description?"

He gave me a look. "I'm your Magic Godfather."

I stared at him, incapable of making words for several seconds. "My what?"

"Magic Godfather." He said the words slowly, like he was trying to help my mind wrap itself around the information.

"One, I wasn't aware that Magic Godfathers existed, and two, I didn't know I had one."

"That's kind of the point. If we went around advertising our services, everyone would know who we are and what we could do, and we wouldn't be much help."

"How long have you been my Magic Godfather?"

He lifted a shoulder. "Since you were born."

How had I never been told about this? I'd never met Kerry until I ran away from my uncle Robert. Kerry was the first person I met my first night alone when I was seeking shelter, and he introduced me to the tunnels and showed me the building I later turned into Haven. "Does everyone have a Magic Godfather?"

"Not everyone, but your parents made sure you did."

"My parents?"

"They didn't know if you had magic when you were born, but they hired me as a precaution. They had me spell your bedroom to make sure you'd always be safe. None of us considered that there might ever be a threat to them as well. I'm sorry I wasn't able to save them too."

I stared at him again, my eyes blurring. "You're the reason my uncle's shifter didn't take me away that night?"

He nodded in a matter of fact way, like it wasn't even a big deal. My heart felt like it was going to burst. All of the emotions I'd been feeling seemed to crash into me at once and I flung myself at Kerry, wrapping my arms around his neck, tears falling silently down my cheeks. "Thank you for saving me."

"I always will, El. Always. I know you've felt alone for a long time, but you never were, I promise. I'm so proud of the woman you've become and how you use your powers. Your mom and dad would have been proud too."

I wiped tears as I stepped back, looking at the scene. My cousins and uncle on the ground, and my friends at my side. "What are we going to do with them?" I asked.

"The Mystic Commission is on its way and they'll take care of your uncle and cousins," Charming said. "Aside from kidnapping, they've broken several laws regarding magic harnessing and transferring. They'll be locked away somewhere they can't hurt you anymore."

His words were like a balm for a wound that had been gaping open for years.

"Thank you," I said, the release overwhelming me and lifting a heavy weight off of my chest.

"You're welcome."

I looked at Sway and Perry, relief shining through my tears. "Let's go home."

CHAPTER 6

*I*t had been a week since the Mystic Ball and the confrontation with my uncle. Charming was right. The Mystic Commission worked swiftly and had judged my uncle and cousins to be a severe threat. They were sent away to a prison specially built to contain mages in another state. Things had started to get back to normal at home. There were rumors swirling about Hadley Scott, the fiery eyed girl in blue who showed up at the Mystic Ball. I knew it was only a matter of time before I had to accept my place as a mage and live in the open with my powers. But I'd keep it a secret as long as I could. It was a relief to know that I was safe, and so were the people I cared about. I had my friends who were basically family, my own powers, and I had my very own Magic Godfather looking after me just in case I ever came across a situation I couldn't handle on my own. Charming had followed through on his word. Haven, and all of the people who lived there with me, had a security team. It hadn't helped much at the ball, but I'd take all the extra protection I could get to keep my friends safe.

The fall day was unseasonably warm on my walk home from work. As I passed one of my favorite parks, I decided to sit by the lake and reflect on everything that had happened during the past two weeks. The sky was pale blue, dusted with clouds, and the lake was a calm sheen, fish swimming peacefully below the surface while ducks floated aimlessly above.

I sat there and thought about life. Two weeks ago, I'd been living the same way I always had—fighting to reach a goal, fighting to stay alive and keep the people I loved safe. I hadn't known Charming, or revealed myself in the magic world. Now a simple stolen shoe had changed everything. The threats were gone for now, but as life went on and people realized Hadley Scott was actually Cinder, new threats would emerge. I'd gone back to work, and things in my universe had calmed down. For the first time in my life, I wasn't worried about who might be looking for me, or about spending all of my extra time searching for my parents' killers. I'd found the man who sent the shifter that had killed my parents, and murdered the friends of Charming's sister. According to Charming, the shifter had been located and subdued by the Hurston family security team. I reached my goal, and now I wasn't sure what to do with myself. My life had been so focused on one task—finding out who took my family from me—that I no longer knew my purpose. Maybe it was time for me to start living for me, instead of living for revenge.

My thoughts strayed to Charming. After we'd left my uncle's house, he'd called to check on me a couple of times. But that's the only contact we'd had. I wasn't sure what to think about that. There was definitely chemistry and a connection between us, and our kiss at the ball had heated me from the inside out before I'd pulled away because I didn't want to end up heartbroken. If everything I'd heard about him was true, he wasn't the relationship type. I'd never even allowed myself to think of a relationship before because I'd been so focused on finding my parents' murderers. Now that was taken care of, but the thought of starting a relationship for the first time, especially with someone like Charming—egotistical, stubborn, challenging, and so freaking hot, terrified me. Could I handle a relationship? Could Charming and I really make one work?

The glass-like surface of the lake was suddenly dotted with drops and fish started jumping. I looked up and saw a tall form, carved arms, and wide shoulders before my eyes landed on his perfect face. Charming was standing five feet from me with a bag of fish food.

It was like I conjured him out of thin air by thinking about him.

"Hi," I said carefully, wondering what he was doing here.

"Hi," he said back. "Come here often?" His eyebrow went up and then one corner of his lips slid into that alluring smile I'd come to think of far too often.

I stared at him. "That's a horrible line."

"It wasn't a line. I'm genuinely curious."

I looked out at the lake and the fish waiting for their benefactor to drop more food. "Sometimes I stop on my way home from work. It's a good place to think."

He inclined his head. "What are you thinking about?"

Him, but I wasn't about to admit that. "Life."

He dropped some more fish food and then moved toward me, sitting next to me on the bench. Less than three inches separated his leg from mine and so help me, I wanted to close the distance and feel his arms wrapped around me again. "Do those thoughts include anyone else?"

I narrowed my eyes. What was he getting at? "Like my friends?"

He leaned back against the bench and stretched an arm

behind me. "Them too. But I was mostly thinking about me. Us."

I blinked. "*Should* my life thoughts and plans include you?"

He fixed his eyes on mine and I couldn't look away. "Do you want them to?"

It felt like butterflies had started a party in my stomach and my heart sped up. I lifted my shoulder, unsure how to answer. Yes, I wanted to see what this was between us. I wanted to have a relationship. But Charming wasn't the relationship type and I'd had enough heartbreak in my life.

"Why did you pull away from our kiss at the ball?" he asked.

I looked at him for several seconds before answering, "Do you want the truth?"

"I always want the truth."

I looked down, composing my thoughts before meeting his eyes. "You're rich, privileged, and you have a reputation for being a spoiled playboy. I doubt you've ever had someone say no to you in your life."

"That's not true," he said, his tone mildly amused. "You've said no repeatedly, and kicked me with your shoe."

I gave him a look. "You deserved the kick."

He tilted his head and I couldn't tell if it was in agreement, or dissent. "The gossip columns aren't the best place to get accurate information about me. I dated a lot when I was younger, but I graduated with my master's degree a few years ago and I've been working with my parents, learning the family business. I go out occasionally with clients and take a date, but it's nothing serious. I haven't had a relationship in a long time. I haven't wanted one." He paused, holding my gaze. "Until now."

I stared at him, eyes wide. I hadn't been expecting that

declaration, or his directness. It took me a minute to recover before I could answer. "I already told you that we come from two different worlds. I'm not used to your world, and don't know if it's the life I want. The magic world is full of power and politics. It's not a world I've ever been interested in. I'm happy in the tunnels with my friends. I could keep being happy there."

He stared at the water for a long time, his face a calm mask. After several minutes he said, "You've spent your whole life trying to get revenge, and helping others. Your friends will always be there for you, that doesn't have to change, regardless of what else you choose to do in life, or with your magic. I hate to be the one to break this to you, but you might not have a choice about becoming part of the magic world. You were the talk of the ball, Hadley—or Ella," he said, raising an eyebrow in question. I didn't have an answer for him. "The hotel had security cameras that caught your magic on video. My security team was able to isolate the recordings, but we don't know who saw them before we did, or if there are any other copies. At some point, you're going to have to declare your powers." He turned to me, his eyes clear. "I'd like to be there to help you navigate the waters of the magic world when you do."

My heart surged at his admission. "Why?"

He licked his lips slowly, a wet sheen of temptation left behind. "I know what it felt like dancing with you, and then outside on the balcony. I've never felt that with anyone else. I want you in my life, El. If you want to be part of it."

I looked up and met his gaze. "I haven't had an easy life, Storm, and I've had enough heartbreak to last a lifetime. How do I know you're telling the truth and you're not going to hurt me?"

He pressed his lips together like he was thinking and then

said, "I can't promise you I'll never hurt you, but I can promise you I'll do my best not to."

I wasn't sure if that promise was enough.

"Test me," he said.

"What?"

"Strip away the illusion and see who I really am, El. See if you can trust me, and if you want to be with me."

Striping the illusion away could be a painful process, or a pleasant one, depending on who the person was, and how much they'd lied to themselves. It wasn't something I did lightly. "You don't know what you're asking. It might not be a pleasant experience, Storm. Most people can't handle who they really are."

"I can," he said immediately. "Test me."

I bit my lip, studying him. He wasn't going to let this go. "Okay," I said. "There's a garden on the other side of the park that's enclosed and private. We can do it there."

We walked together and when we came to the entrance we went through a tunnel of flowers and leaves that opened up into a quiet, serene garden fragrant with blooming flowers and freshly turned soil. It was one of my favorite parts of the park. We stood on an area with brick pavers and I looked into his eyes, searching for any hint of reticence. I found a calm and quiet confidence instead. "Are you ready?"

He nodded.

I closed my eyes and raised my hands, letting my magic push onto him. The flames rose around him, a brilliant blue, before the cinders from his illusion scattered to the ground. I gathered them, and pushed them toward him. Then waited for Charming's mirror to appear. It did, and what it reflected back shocked me. It was Charming, helping others, caring for animals, speaking for those who couldn't speak for themselves. He was good, and he was kind, and I knew he really would try not to hurt me. And I realized the truth was I hadn't needed my illusion breaking magic to tell me that. The only thing holding me back from him was fear, and I'd never let fear rule my life before. I wasn't about to start now.

He reached out and took my hands in his, the touch warm and reassuring. "Be with me."

I looked up at him, emotion clouding my vision, and flung my arms around his neck. His strong arms went around my back and I was sheltered and safe and my heart felt like it might burst in my chest. His lips found mine and told me everything my magic already had. This was a man who was truly good, and would do anything to make me happy. It was something I hadn't even realized I'd wanted, but now I didn't want to imagine life without it.

A gust of wind picked up and Storm used his magic to sweep the glass into a trash can. One piece fell to the ground. I bent to pick it up and looked at it, then started to laugh. Charming's brow went up with interest as he looked over my shoulder and then started laughing too. It was a picture of my shoe. "So you're not all good, Charming. Even my magic knows you're a thief."

The smile he flashed me could have lit up an entire city. "I'd happily do it all over again if it meant I got to meet you."

My cheeks pinked and joy washed through me like a ray of white light. I put my arms around his neck and he returned the favor, wrapping his arms around my waist. "You were right," I said.

One of his eyebrows rose. "About what?"

"You said one day I'd ask you to capture me. I'm asking you now."

The corners of his lips kicked up. "And I'm never letting you go." His lips met mine and with them, the weight that had been on my shoulders my whole life lifted, carried by two instead of one.

Charming took my hand and I followed him through the

garden tunnel and out into the world and our happily ever after.

The End

ABOUT THE AUTHOR

Angela Corbett graduated from Westminster College and previously worked as a journalist, freelance writer, and director of communications and marketing. She lives in Utah with her extremely supportive husband, and loves classic cars, traveling, and chasing their five-pound Pomeranian, Pippin—who is just as mischievous as his hobbit namesake. She's the author of Young Adult, New Adult, and Adult fiction—with lots of kissing. She writes under two names, Angela Corbett, and Destiny Ford.

http://www.angelacorbett.com/

Join my newsletter to get a free book!
http://eepurl.com/KhLAn

facebook.com/AuthorAngelaCorbett

twitter.com/angcorbett

instagram.com/byangcorbett